SING SWEETLY TO ME

Twisted minds are Margie Reed's business —she is a forensic psychologist who specialises in looking for the dark reasons behind criminal behaviour. Alone in her apartment, working in her office, walking to her car, she knows someone is watching. Then come the flowers. And the warnings. Someone has already killed and now he wants her to die. One brave police officer believes Margie can help him catch the pyschopath but only if she dares to face what lurks in the shadows...

SING SWEETLY TO ME

SING SWEETLY TO ME

by

Barbara Pronin

Magna Large Print Books
Long Preston, North Yorkshire,
England.

British Library Cataloguing in Publication Data.

Pronin, Barbara
Sing sweetly to me.

A catalogue record for this book is
available from the British Library

ISBN 0-7505-0889-2

First published in Great Britain by Judy Piatkus (Publishers)
Ltd., 1992

Published in Large Print October, 1995 by arrangement with
Barbara Pronin.

Magna Large Print is an imprint of
Library Magna Books Ltd.
Printed and bound in Great Britain by
T.J. Press (Padstow) Ltd., Cornwall, PL28 8RW.

For Joe

For Joe

For their kindness in sharing knowledge and expertise with me, I am grateful to Rob Welborn, Dr Gil Martin, and, most especially, to Reneau Kennedy, whose love of her work was truly the start of the story.

PROLOGUE

Vejar State Hospital
Santa Barbara, California
September 23

It was stuffy in the doctor's office and Denny wanted out, but he forced himself to focus his attention on the man who would make the decision.

The doctor was puffing on an unlit pipe, tapping his fingers on a stack of folders to no rhythm Denny recognized. He was fat, balding, and pasty-faced, but Denny knew he must listen to him carefully and be prepared to answer questions.

'From a medical standpoint,' the doctor said at last, 'there seems to be no reason to keep you, Mr'—he looked again at the file—'Kiefer, is it?'

'Kiefer, yes, sir, Denny Kiefer. I have to tell you, I feel great, Dr Landesmann, I really feel just fine.'

'Mmm,' the doctor said, not seeming to hear as he consulted the topmost folder. 'Dizziness, nausea, vomiting gone, etcetera, etcetera, etcetera. Well, it seems, Mr Kiefer, that whatever you ingested is successfully out of your system.'

'Yes, sir, absolutely,' Denny nodded. 'I surely do feel fine. And I have to get out of here, Dr Landesmann. There's this job—in Coos Bay, Oregon?'

'Mmm...'

Denny patted the pocket of his windbreaker and looked earnestly at the doctor. 'See, I have this letter here from my cousin. There's a job waiting for me at the lumber mill.'

The doctor looked directly at Denny, his puffy eyes narrowed. 'I don't know where you came from Mr Kiefer, and I don't know where you're going. But there are some on this staff who are recommending that discharging you would be precipitous. They are suggesting you might benefit from a period of psychiatric observation.'

Denny willed the prickling of sweat to leave his upper lip. 'Dr Landesmann,' he said, looking straight at the doctor, 'I deeply regret that—outburst. I never intended to lose my temper with Nurse Whiting the other day. I have apologized to her, sir. I—hoped she understood. I hope you do as well. And, sir, it is very important to me that I get on up to Coos Bay.'

The doctor looked away, frowning slightly as he perused the chart once more.

12

Denny could feel the tension building in that place behind his eyes. *Steady*, he told himself. *You're almost there*. He could feel the doctor wavering.

'Oregon, eh? That's a long way. How do you plan to get there?'

Denny was prepared. 'My cousin,' he said, patting his jacket pocket. 'He's sending me money for bus fare. He mailed it to me, in fact, care of General Delivery, here in Santa Barbara. It's probably waiting for me now at the Post Office. I just have to pick it up.'

'Mmm.' The doctor peered at him again, drumming his fingers on the desk. The phone rang. 'Dr Landesmann here. Yes, yes, I'll be right there.'

The doctor scribbled something on the chart and laid it aside on the desk. Then, taking a card from his desk drawer, he scrawled something on the back. Heaving his bulk up from the leather chair, he handed the card to Denny.

'Your discharge order will be waiting downstairs. Sign out at the desk. If you need a bed or whatever before you get out of town, here's the address of a shelter.'

Denny was on his feet. 'Dr Landesmann, thank you. I'll send you a card from Oregon.'

But the doctor was distracted, opening the door, motioning the patient out. Denny needed no second invitation. He heard the door close behind him.

In a moment, listening to the satisfying squish of his sneakers on the polished floor, he was at the elevator, pushing the button, moving into the car.

He shared the ride down with two student nurses, pretty, but he didn't care. He bolted from the elevator, strode across the lobby and out into the open air.

The sea breeze bit through his windbreaker and caused him to shiver some. He moved purposefully away from the entrance to the seaward side of the building.

He found himself on a deserted greenbelt that stretched out toward the ocean. *Trust the state*, he thought, *to build the hospital ass backwards to the view*. Filling his lungs with damp air, he considered what to do next.

Thirty feet away against the hospital wall a gardener was hunched over a flower bed, tossing weeds back over his shoulder with a steady, noiseless rhythm. Denny looked up. There were no windows on the lower floors of the building. It would be impossible for anyone looking out to see directly below.

Slowly he edged his way along the wall toward a wheelbarrow filled with tools. Lifting a sturdy, earth-covered shovel, he moved quickly toward the gardener until he was near enough to raise his arms and deliver a skull-crushing blow.

14

With a single cry the gardener pitched forward, then sprawled across the ground, a thin trickle of blood running down behind his ear to mingle with the red adobe soil.

Poised to run, Denny glanced once around. He tossed aside the shovel. Convinced it was safe, he leaned across the dead man and plucked his wallet from his pocket.

A green card inside identified the gardener as Ramon José Garcia. He was twenty-four years old, the same age as Denny, birthplace Sonora, Mexico. Folded behind the card were three crumpled fives and six one-dollar bills.

Denny stuffed the bills into the pocket of his jeans. He thought about keeping the green card, but then he realized that with his blond hair and blue eyes, it was unlikely he could ever pass as a registered alien named Garcia.

Instead, he tugged at a thin chain that hung from the gardener's neck and deposited it, tarnished silver cross and all, in his jacket pocket. Tossing the wallet into the flower bed, he moved casually past the hospital entrance. Then he picked up speed, sprinted across the parking lot, and turned left on Coast Highway.

He was careful to keep his arms at that

peculiar angle runners seemed to favour. No one would remember a young guy jogging less than a mile from the campus. By the time he reached the university, he knew what he was going to do.

In the library he blended easily among the students browsing in the stacks. It didn't take long to spot what he wanted—an unattended book bag. Hoisting it over his left shoulder, he made a beeline for the door.

Someone was yelling from the library steps. Denny picked up his pace, gliding through clutches of milling students in a serpentine path across the campus.

It was only when he reached the Coast Highway that he turned to look behind him. No one had followed. He was perfectly safe. He paused to catch his breath, then held the book bag aloft, the university logo facing traffic. The fifth driver heading south slowed and braked to a stop.

Denny slung the book bag over his shoulder and jogged over to the grey Cutlass, whose driver peered at him as an automatic window slid down.

'Say there, preppie, where ya headed?'

'L.A, sir—if you're going that far. I really have to get home.'

'You do, eh? What's your hurry? Seems like school just started.'

'Yes, sir. It's my dad. He's had a heart attack. My mother called. I have to get home.'

'I see.' The driver was silent a moment, as if he were sizing Denny up. Then he hit a button. The passenger door lock popped up. 'Get in. We'll have you home in no time.'

Grinning, Denny slipped off the wind-breaker and stuffed it in a compartment of the book bag. He threw the bag in the back seat and climbed into the Cutlass. 'Thank you, sir.' He extended a hand. 'I appreciate this. God bless you...'

CHAPTER 1

Santa Clarita Valley
Northwest of Los Angeles
September 28

It had been a pleasant evening, Margie admitted, slipping into her nightgown. Chet had promised a nice quiet dinner, and that was what they'd shared, along with a glass of wine, a joke or two, and good conversation.

There was no mistaking the look in his eyes as they'd said good night at her door, though Chet had not pressed her when Margie made it clear that she wasn't ready for more.

Pinning her dark curls back with a barrette, she dipped a cotton pad into a jar of cold cream and began to remove her makeup. Then she stopped, staring dolefully at the sombre face in the mirror.

It seemed to Margie that her hazel eyes had darkened to an austere brown, and tiny lines had begun to form in the middle part of her brow. She was only twenty-eight, but the lines were there and she found it disconcerting.

Tilting her face, she forced a smile and peered out from under thick lashes. It gave her face a playful look and made her look years younger. That was the Margie she remembered best, the Margie she could be again. She might not be ready for another romance, but she would make an effort to smile.

She found the simple promise cheering and smiled again at her reflection. Then she brushed her teeth, turned out the lights, and slipped between the sheets.

She woke with a start, her heart pounding. Had she heard someone scream? Or was it the nightmare, back to haunt her, her own cries echoing in her head?

Margie sat up in bed, her eyes wide, seeing nothing in the darkness. She listened, but there was no sound except the wind in the trees outside her window.

Aware that she was holding her breath, she let it out slowly and sank back on one elbow to look at her bedside clock. Twelve twenty. She'd not been asleep long. It must have been the dream that woke her...but it had seemed so real. She flung off the blanket and rose unsteadily to her feet.

Pulling on a robe, she moved slowly toward the door and leaned against it, listening. Then she unlocked it and opened it as far as the chain and bolt would allow.

Surely, if she had heard a scream, others would have heard it, too. But the corridor was empty as far as she could see, the doors across the hallway closed.

Bolder now, she undid the chain and opened her door wide, padding barefoot to the open stairwell to peer over the banister. There was no one there. It must have been a nightmare. She straightened up to go back in.

She was halfway inside when a sudden impulse made her turn her head and look up. She stared for a moment into the empty upper landing until the feeling passed.

Inside, she locked and bolted the door and wavered for a minute by the phone, debating whether to call the police or admit she had simply had a nightmare.

Unsure, she went to her bedroom window and pulled aside the curtain— which, she realized, she should have done in the first place instead of prowling around in the hall. She looked down through the trees into the brick-lined square below, the common courtyard to the complex of apartment buildings she'd found not far from the state hospital.

The courtyard was lighted by a double row of gas lamps that extended to the parking garage. But as far as Margie could see, there was no one out there, nothing moving at all, except a few swirls of liquid amber leaves caught in the gusting draughts.

It was September, and warm, the season for Santa Anas—hot, dry winds that blow up from Mexico and howl through the streets of Southern California as though they were still open plains. Margie was new to the Santa Clarita Valley, and the four distinct seasons that characterized upper Connecticut were still fresh in her memory. But already she recognized these desertlike winds that seemed to hold winter at bay.

She glanced up, searching rows of windows, thinking she might see someone else at the curtains who had been wakened by the noise she thought she'd heard. But the windows were either dark or muted patches of light, revealing nothing of the neighbours she did not know, though she'd lived here for nearly six months.

Finally she looked beyond the apartments toward the lights of Santa Clarita State Hospital. Perhaps it was the wail of a siren she'd heard. Yes, that could have been it.

Sighing, Margie dropped the curtain in place and turned back to her bed. But she was wide awake, too much so to sleep. Maybe a cup of tea would help.

She could see quite clearly in the

darkness by now, but she turned on the kitchen light anyway. She put water on to boil and got down her favourite mug, the heavy blue one Trisha had made for her last Christmas, before—when they had all been together.

Determined not to upset herself even more, Margie concentrated on her sister-in-law. Pretty Trisha. How she wished she could see her now. How happy she must be with the baby. She was picturing that when the telephone rang, a sharp shrill that sent her blood pressure soaring for the second time in an hour.

'Hello—'

'Marg? It's me, Rob.'

'Oh, Rob, you scared me to death! I was just thinking of Trisha and the baby—' Margie stopped herself. It was nearly four in the morning in Connecticut. 'Rob, is someth—what's wrong?'

Her brother sighed. 'It's Trisha. She's gone. She took the baby and left. I probably woke you. I'm sorry, Marg. I didn't know what else to do.'

Margie frowned. 'Where are you, Rob? When did Trisha leave?'

'I'm home. I just got here and found a note. I guess she left sometime tonight.'

Margie did not ask him why he'd only just come home in the wee hours of the morning. 'Did you argue or something? I mean, a person doesn't leave without any warning at all.'

Rob paused. 'No, we didn't argue. Not recently, anyway. I—well, okay, she's threatened once or twice....'

'Threatened what? To leave?'

'Yes. I didn't think she'd do it, though. God, Margie, she knows I love her. Anyway, I doubt she's gone far. I just—I thought maybe she'd called you.'

'No, Rob. I haven't heard from her.'

'Will you call me if you do?'

'Of course. I'm sure she'd want you to know that she and the baby are all right. Meanwhile, in the morning, check with her friends. You're probably right, she hasn't gone far...' Margie hesitated. This was not the time to ask what the two of them had argued about. 'And listen, Rob, you call me back the minute you know they're okay.'

'I will.'

'Okay. I love you, Rob.'

'I love you, too. 'Night, Marg.'

The water had boiled down to a scant mugful by the time Margie got back to it. She poured the tea and took it to the window, scanning the landscape again. A lone jogger on the outer perimeter of the complex headed toward the highway. A hospital orderly on the graveyard shift, she supposed, or someone unwinding before bedtime. That was another thing Margie had noticed. Everybody in California jogged.

She sipped the tea, relishing its fragrance, knowing she should go back to bed. She was seeing the Walters boy tomorrow and she would want to be fresh and alert. But if the scream—or the nightmare—hadn't wakened her, Rob's phone call would have. Either way, she was fully awake, and now there was Trisha to worry about.

Wrapping her hands around the warmth of the mug, she thought again of last Christmas. The four of them had been so happy in that rented cabin in the Berkshires.

It had snowed most of the day, a dry powder, the temperature well below freezing. They'd been grateful to get the groceries unpacked and a roaring fire started.

Rob, married just over a year and a solicitous father-to-be, had settled Trisha comfortably in a rocker. Margie and Frank had pulled on their parkas and gone for a walk in the woods.

New snow nestled in the branches above their heads and crunched under their boots, and sunlight glancing off the white landscape gave it an iridescent glow. Margie breathed in the pine-scented cold and returned Frank's happy smile, thinking how impossible it seemed that six months earlier she had not even known him.

They had met in a Hartford courtroom while working on the same case; Frank was the prosecutor and Margie was brought in as a state psychologist in a case involving malicious mischief and aggravated assault against a local farmer. Frank argued that the defendant, Roy Gates, had premeditated the acts of violence, while the defence claimed Gates was a hapless victim of mental illness.

Margie, after a thorough analysis, concluded that Gates was cunning but sane, an organized sociopath who planned his attacks and most certainly should stand trial. But neither her testimony nor Frank's arguments had been enough to send him to prison. Gates had drawn a stint at a state hospital, and that had been the end of it.

For Margie and Frank it was the beginning of a friendship that had quickly become much more, and now, matching her stride to his, it seemed she had known him always. She felt that if the world should stop, this was where she'd want to be.

'This is God's country,' Frank whispered, putting her thoughts into words. 'There's a peacefulness here like nowhere else. If I thought I could make a living here, I'd stay.'

Margie burrowed closer to him. 'You

could, if you really wanted to. Even in the mountains, people need attorneys.'

Frank shook his head. 'And be a desk jockey? No, that's not for me. I love the courtroom; you know that, Margie.'

'Yes, my love, I do. You thrive on the excitement, the high drama.'

'Okay, so I should have been an actor.'

Margie smiled. 'Not for a minute. You're too darn good at what you do.'

'Right,' Frank said. 'Defender of justice. Trying to outswim the sharks.'

They paused to watch a pair of grey squirrels forage in a fallen tree trunk, then scamper off with a light-footed grace that barely left tracks in the snow.

'I've got it,' Frank said. 'We'll have two houses, one in the city and one here. Then, when we get fed up with the sharks, we can hide up here with the squirrels.'

'And run like rabbits from the big, bad wolf who wants to collect on the mortgages.'

Frank laughed, a deep chuckle that echoed in the silence, and drew Margie to him until their faces met and the smile faded from his lips. 'Marry me, Margie. I love you so much. I want to spend the rest of my life with you.'

Margie shivered with joy and cold. 'Nothing would make me happier.'

They held each other for a long moment,

oblivious to the cold. Then the wind picked up and a dusting of snow began to swirl about their heads.

'Race you to the cabin,' Frank said, swatting her gently on the rump.

'No fair! Your legs are longer,' Margie shouted, already beginning to run. 'I get a handicap, and the first one there gets to tell Rob and Trish the news!'

The day was as clear and sharp in her memory as if it happened yesterday, etched into her brain like the letters of her name on the blue mug now cold in her hands.

Exhausted, Margie set down the mug and crawled back into bed. It was no good remembering. She had done the right thing when she accepted the offer in California.

Eventually, beset with fragmented images, she fell into a restless sleep, only to wake at the howl of the wind and stare into the night.

CHAPTER 2

The morning was bright and cloudless, Margie saw as she drove the two-mile distance to the hospital. There was no hint of last night's wind except that the range of mountains to the north stood out in relief against the pale blue sky, evidence that the Santa Ana winds had swept through and cleared away the smog.

The mountains were a dull grey-brown and craggy, not at all like the Berkshire Hills she loved. Still, they were majestic in their own Spartan way, and Margie wished she could enjoy this rare glimpse of them. But lack of sleep and fragmented dreams had taken a heavy toll, and the Tylenol she'd taken before breakfast had not yet made a dent in her headache.

She was worried about Rob and Trisha and the baby and wondered when she would hear from them. More than that, she realized in the clear light of the day, it was increasingly hard to convince herself that what had awakened her last night had been anything but a woman's scream.

I should have called the police, she told herself, *that's what I should have done, if for no other reason than that they might have looked around and assured me that everything was okay.* An argument, maybe, between two roommates. Who knew why people screamed?

But she hadn't called, and now she would feel silly, calling in to report she'd heard a scream more than eight hours ago.

She drove into the employees' lot at

Santa Clarita State Hospital, manoeuvering the Honda past the choicest parking spots to a walled area out of sight of the prison ward where staff psychologists were asked to park.

On the face of it, she realized, it was a reasonable precaution, given the fact that the prisoners she dealt with could be back out on the streets at any time. On most mornings, in fact, she did not mind the extra walk. When the weather was good, she almost welcomed it, but today she was impatient to get to her office. Silly or not, she was going to make that call.

The building was old, worn, and cavernous, echoing with the sounds of the sick and the desperate, and smelling somehow faintly of mildew despite its daily scrubbings.

Margie took an elevator to the eleventh floor, one floor below the topmost level, which was in such disrepair that it was no longer used for patients.

The eleventh was bad enough, with its yellowing walls and an accumulation of forty years' worth of steam table smells seeping up from the cafeteria below.

Margie strode past the worst of the food smells, past a small, makeshift library, and stopped at a heavy metal door at the far end of the hall. Stretching to her full height to peer through a small square of safety glass, she pressed the buzzer at one side of the door and waited for Mack to buzz her in.

'Morning!' Mack greeted her with his customary good cheer. 'Ah, you're a sight for sore eyes!'

Margie smiled ruefully. 'Don't look too close. I'm not at my scintillating best.'

Mack winked at her. 'Late night?'

'Short night. I didn't get much sleep.'

She continued past him to her small office halfway down the corridor, at the end of which a double set of doors led to a dozen cells.

Tossing her linen jacket over the back of a chair, she glanced at the Walters file, pulled for her to read before the interview she was to have with the new patient this morning. She was anxious to read it, but she put it aside and reached for a telephone book. Scanning it for the number of the Santa Clarita Sheriff's office, she picked up the telephone and punched the numbers quickly, before she could change her mind.

A youthful voice came on the line. 'Desk, Sergeant Jordan. Can I help you?'

'I hope so,' Margie said. 'My name is Margie Reed. I'm a psychologist at Santa Clarita State Hospital. I live not far from here, in the Wentworth Apartments, on Wentworth just north of the boulevard.'

'Yes, ma'am.' The voice urged her along, but Margie took her time.

'Last night, about twelve twenty—actually, I suppose it was twelve twenty this morning—I heard—well, I thought I heard a woman scream.'

'At the hospital?'

'No, Sergeant. At home.' Margie paused. 'I should have reported it right away. But I—I thought at first I might have been dreaming. I was asleep, you see. The sound woke me. And then I thought maybe I'd dreamed it.'

'Uh-huh.'

The officer was being less than helpful, and Margie began to feel foolish. 'Anyway,' she said, 'the more I thought about it, the surer I became that it was real. Someone screamed. I only heard it once, but I feel certain it was a scream.'

'I see,' the officer said flatly. 'Could you tell where the noise was coming from?'

'Near my apartment. I went out to look around, but I didn't see or hear anything.'

'No one in the area who didn't belong there?'

'No. I didn't see anyone.'

The officer paused. 'No further disturbance?'

'No...not to my knowledge.'

'Well, ma'am, if you had called last night, we would have sent a car to look around.'

'I appreciate that, Sergeant. I guess I'm just wondering if you knew of any trouble in the area.'

'Checking the blotter, ma'am, I find no record of any reports from that neighbourhood. If it will make you feel better, I can send a car tonight, or have the day patrol cruise by.'

Margie sighed. 'Whatever you think. If there's no record of any trouble...'

'Well, ma'am, we thank you for calling. We'll certainly have a look around.'

'Officer, it's a big complex. I live in building two, apartment three-B.'

'Well, I doubt we'll be knocking on any doors. But I'll dispatch a car to cruise the area.'

'Thank you, Sergeant.'

'No problem at all.' The call was disconnected.

Fat lot of good that did, Margie thought, replacing the phone on the hook. *My own fault. I should have called last night. But then, there'd been nothing reported. Maybe I did dream the whole thing. Maybe I should mind my own business.*

Resting her chin on her hand for a moment, she put the thought firmly out of mind. She reached for the file marked

'Walters, Glenn,' and opened it to read the court order.

Her new patient was an eighteen-year-old Caucasian male with no prior adult record, who had come to California some months ago with his family from Scottsdale, Arizona.

He was charged with the torture of a Siamese cat, which had been disembowelled and left in its owner's mailbox. The owner, a seventy-two-year old woman, had suffered a heart attack upon finding the corpse and was still under hospital care.

Margie recalled that the story had made banner headlines, understandably arousing wrath and fear in a quiet, suburban neighbourhood. It had been several weeks before the Walters boy had been arrested, but his arraignment had been widely covered. At a pretrial hearing, the judge had ordered psychological reports on Glenn's competence to stand trial and, concurrently, on his mental state at the time of the alleged offence.

Margie made a note to check for juvenile records in Scottsdale, Arizona. With a crime of this nature, it was very likely the boy had some previous history. She was about to read the lengthy police report when the telephone sounded at her elbow. She barely had time to identify herself before a voice bellowed into her ear.

'Good morning! This is Carlton Richards, attorney for Glenn Walters. I've just been retained to represent the young man and I wondered if you'd seen him yet.'

'No, I haven't,' Margie said. 'I'll be seeing him later this morning.'

Richards growled. 'Totally ridiculous! There's no need for mental evaluation. A childish little prank has been blown out of proportion and the court sends him to you!'

'That's what I'm here for,' Margie said, mildly surprised at Richards's tactic. 'This "childish little prank" is a felony, after all, and a woman has suffered a heart attack.'

'Elderly people are subject to heart attacks—it simply comes with the territory. Glenn Walters did not intentionally or unintentionally cause her to suffer this one.'

They were getting into the legal arena, and Margie was not about to be drawn in. 'Tell me, Mr Richards, do you happen to know if your client has a juvenile record?'

'I do not,' Richards said. 'I was only retained by Glenn's parents this morning. In any case, it has no relevance to the case currently pending.'

It was clear she would get nothing more from Richards, who had undoubtedly not yet seen his client. She had work to do and she wanted to get on with it. 'Well, thank you for calling, Mr Richards. If there's nothing else, I'll be in touch as I gather information.'

The attorney paused. 'I thought I should tell you I am considering moving Glenn to a private psychiatric facility. I thought, inasmuch as the court has ordered these reports, perhaps a private psychologist—'

'You have that option,' Margie said. 'I'm sure you know the procedure.'

'Yes. Well, we'll see. We'll certainly see.' The phone went dead in Margie's hand.

Nurse Emma Danziger glanced at the clock and rubbed her blistered left heel. Damned if she'd buy sale shoes again for the miles she put on around here.

She should have listened to Lilly Platz. The pace up here was insane—patients in and out like a revolving door—you'd think it was a damned hotel, and the doctors so rushed even she had trouble reading their orders on the charts.

Deftly avoiding a fast-moving gurney, she made her way down the hall. One quick check of the sixth-floor beds and she was on her way to lunch at last.

There was an empty bed in 6114. Emma stopped to think. She could swear a patient had been assigned there an hour ago, complaining of some kind of food poisoning.

Three other patients were sound asleep: no help coming from them. She limped in, looking for a chart, but it had not yet arrived on the ward. No surprise, Emma thought, the way things got done around here. Well, she would look for it at the nurses' station before she went to lunch.

She finished the bed check and, favouring her sore foot, made her way back up the hall, where three women dressed in East Indian saris were clustered around a baffled-looking Lilly.

'They keep telling me they're ready,' Lilly said. 'But I don't know for what!'

Emma listened to the women's chatter. 'Red-dy...Am-rit Reddy...'

'They're looking for Amrit Reddy, Lilly, the colostomy in sixty-one fifty. I'm out of here, okay? I'm going to lunch.' She retrieved her purse from a file cabinet.

The elevator was halfway up to the cafeteria before she remembered the empty bed.

Margie had read the police report on Walters and was making some preliminary notes when she heard Chet Anderson's familiar whistle somewhere out in the hall. A moment later the blond psychologist leaned into her doorway, pushing his glasses up on his nose and smiling his cherubic smile.

'If I read it right, it's after ten. Time for coffee, eh?'

'Sure,' Margie said. 'I have this raging headache. A little caffeine is called for.'

They took the stairs to the floor below and stood in line for coffee, carrying it to a table on the far side of the cafeteria, away from most of the noise.

'Wish I had a cheese Danish,' Chet said, biting into a doughnut.

'I hate cheese Danishes.'

'You'd like these. I get them at Harry's Deli. They're great for headaches.'

'I'll bet,' Margie said.

'So where did the headache come from?'

Margie shrugged. 'A bad night and an unendearing lawyer. His name is Richards. Carlton Richards. He's representing Glenn Walters.'

Chet polished off the last of his doughnut. 'Must be money in the family. Richards hangs out in the high rent district. So you got the Walters kid, eh?'

'Yes.' Margie sipped at her hot coffee. 'I'll be seeing him as soon as we're through here. According to Richards, the entire incident was nothing but a childish prank. But I'm not so sure, after reading the police report, and obviously the court isn't, either.'

38

'Any priors?' Chet asked, getting up to refill their cups from a pot that sat on a sideboard.

'Not here,' Margie said. 'But I'm checking with Arizona to see if there's a juvenile file.'

Chet grimaced. 'Good luck getting it, even if it does exist. Heaven forbid they might have made a mistake when they let him slip off their hook.'

'I know,' Margie said. 'But I have a feeling that his history is going to be important. If I have to, I'll go through a juvenile court judge to get the records released.'

Chet nodded. 'If I know Richards, he'll want the kid moved elsewhere. Somewhere very private and very posh with an accommodating private shrink.'

'He's already indicated the possibility.' Margie finished her coffee. 'Maybe he thinks he can buy a report that says what he wants to hear.'

'It wouldn't be the first time.' Chet shrugged. 'And probably not the last.'

'All of which means that my clock is running. I really ought to get back.'

'Right. Margie, I enjoyed last night. I'd like to do it again.'

'Well, it's my treat next time. That's only fair. Your paycheck's no bigger than mine.'

She started to rise but Chet stopped her, placing a hand over hers. 'Hey,' he said, forcing her to look at him. 'Okay, I can see you've been hurt. If you want to tell me what happened, that's fine, and if you don't, that's okay, too. But it's past. This is now. I like you a lot, and I'd like to look ahead.'

Margie saw the warmth in his eyes. She had looked at someone with such tenderness once. 'I've—got to get back,' she said softly.

'I know. But I'm here if you need me.'

CHAPTER 3

Sheriff's Homicide Lieutenant Paul Sellers knelt to look at the body.

The young woman was lying at an angle, clad in a light summer robe. With her eyes closed and her honey-coloured hair splayed out around her face, she looked as though she might be sleeping. But a dark patch of blood on the carpet, surrounded by shards of what had once been a heavy glass vase, gave evidence of the violence that had put her there.

From her position in the doorway between the living room and bedroom,

40

Sellers guessed she had seen her attacker coming. Probably she had tried to retreat, but she had not been quick enough to avoid the blow.

In the absence of signs of forced entry to the apartment, he presumed she had let him in. More often than not, Sellers was aware, the victim knew the assailant.

Soon the homicide team would arrive to check every inch of the apartment, to chalk the position in which the body had been found before the coroner took it for autopsy. This moment, however, was his, and Sellers used it to memorize every feature of her face, as though knowing her better might somehow make it easier to get a beat on her killer.

A few feet away the victim's roommate sobbed quietly on the sofa. When her sobs subsided, the lieutenant rose and moved to sit beside her.

'I'm sorry,' he said, his voice solemn. 'I know this is very hard. It was a terrible shock, to come home and find her. Have you roomed together long?'

The young woman nodded, her eyes red-rimmed as she wiped away fresh tears. 'About a year, first on Madison, and then here at the Wentworth. But like a lot of flight attendants, we didn't see each other much. We were always working different shifts.'

41

'I see. Did you generally know each other's schedules? Would she have known when to expect you home?'

She nodded again. 'She knew I was working a night flight, that I'd be home by nine or so this morning. She probably got home about eleven last night. That is, if she came straight home.'

'Did she usually? Come right home after she left a flight?'

The roommate shrugged, her lower lip quivering as her eyes filled again. 'Sometimes she did, but sometimes at night, she'd stop to have a few drinks. Oh, Lieutenant, I warned her and warned her—'

Sellers was gentle. 'You warned her about what?'

'About bringing guys home! Sometimes if she knew she'd have the place to herself, she'd stop at Sidney's on the boulevard. And then, if some guy struck her fancy, she'd bring him back here with her. I told her someday she'd pick the wrong guy, but Jeannie laughed it off. She was—I don't know what you'd call it, Lieutenant, Jeannie thought she was—invincible.'

'I see,' he said. 'Then Miss Kerns didn't have what you'd call a steady boyfriend?'

'No, not really,' her roommate said. 'She liked a lot of guys. But not for long, for some reason or other. She was always looking for someone new.'

Sellers intended to get a list of the men Jeanne Kerns had known, and to stop at Sidney's to see if anyone remembered if she'd been at the bar last night. But the heavy knock sounding at the door meant the homicide team had arrived, and his first priority was to get this woman out of here so that they could go to work.

He would put in a call to the victim's family, the chore he hated most. Then he intended to see the hospital psychologist Jordan said had called in this morning...

Margie appraised the silent young man sitting across from her desk and tried to decide whether it was a smile or a sneer that played across his lips.

He was slight for his age, light complected, with neatly combed brown hair and dark eyes that stared straight ahead, as though she were not even in the room.

'Glenn,' she said, 'I will be asking you questions about your relationship with your attorney, and also about your understanding of the legal process in this state.'

Glenn's expression did not change. His hostility was almost palpable.

'I will also ask you questions about your present state of mind,' she said, 'and about certain aspects of your past life, particularly the time just before, and just after your arrest.'

Margie explained that what Glenn told her could not be used against him in court, but that it might be used to help the judge decide whether Glenn was able to stand trial.

The young man laughed. 'You mean if I'm sane? You can tell the judge I'm sane. And don't think I believe that other crap, because I don't believe it for a minute.'

'Believe what, Glenn?' Margie asked.

'That it won't be used against me.' He looked at Margie for the first time. 'You shrinks are all alike. You sit there and talk to me for ten minutes and try to decide if I'm crazy. Then you twist everything I say and take it back to court.'

'Sounds like you've seen a lot of shrinks, not to mention a lot of courts.'

'Yeah, well, I'm smart enough to know that if you've seen one, you've seen 'em all!'

'Where did you learn about all this, Glenn, here in Los Angeles or in Scottsdale?'

Glenn glared at her, his smile twisted. 'Wouldn't you like to know?'

'You know you can have your attorney present, if you don't want to talk to me alone.'

Glenn snorted. 'That stupid wimp! I

44

don't need his help, either.'

Margie could not help smiling as she remembered her talk with Carlton Richards. 'I talked with Mr Richards just this morning. He didn't sound wimpy to me.'

Glenn shot her a look. 'Richards? Who's Richards? He wasn't the guy in court.' Then his face twisted into a smile. 'So good, old Mom came through...'

'Came through?' Margie asked. 'You mean you asked your mother to get you a different attorney?'

'Yes, if it's any of your business. I asked for somebody with some smarts, somebody who knows you don't have to be crazy just because you snuffed some stupid cat.'

'Did you kill the cat, Glenn?'

The boy paused. 'Yeah, I killed it. So what?'

'How did you kill it?'

The boy looked right at her. 'I slit its ugly throat. Then I slit it up the middle and took its slimy guts out.'

Margie knew he was trying to shock her. She kept her voice even and calm. 'Why did you kill it? Did you have a reason?'

He shrugged. 'It was just a cat.'

'Even the cat must have cried out in pain. How did you feel about that?'

He looked away. 'I didn't feel anything. It was just a cat, okay?'

45

Margie said nothing. He was very agitated. She could see his muscles tense. Finally, he snarled at her through clenched teeth. 'It was just—a lousy—cat! Jesus, what's the big, damn deal? I didn't kill the old lady!'

Margie watched him, prepared to call for Mack if his agitation moved toward violence. 'If you mean the lady who owned the cat,' she said, 'you know she suffered a heart attack. She's very ill. She may die. Does that bother you at all?'

Glenn seemed to be back in control. He leaned back in his chair. 'I didn't kill her,' he said slowly. 'I could have, if I wanted to, you know. I could have killed the old lady. But I didn't. It was just a cat.'

Margie noted the veiled threat and the total lack of remorse. 'Obviously, you knew it was her cat you killed, because you left it in her mailbox for her to find. Did you know Mrs Hardesty, Glenn? Were you angry with her for some reason?'

Glenn turned away, folded his arms, and refused to look at her again. 'I don't feel like talking anymore,' he said. 'I want to see my new attorney.'

'All right,' she told him. 'That's enough for today. I'll see you again tomorrow. I'm quite sure Mr Richards will be here to see you the very first chance he gets.'

When Glenn didn't respond, Margie

picked up the phone and waited to hear Mack's voice. 'It's me, Mack,' she said. 'I think Mr Walters is ready to go back to his cell.'

In a moment, the guard was at her door. 'All right, young fella, let's go.'

Glenn got up slowly, as if he wanted to show Margie he would do things in his own way. When he was ready, he turned around and sauntered out of the room.

Margie watched his retreating back, recounting what she had learned, for although her session with Glenn had been short, it had been more productive than he knew.

He was egocentric, antisocial, and easily moved toward violence. But Margie believed what he'd told her was true. He was sane enough to stand trial.

Willard Miller parked his grey Cutlass in a half-empty visitors' lot and trekked uphill to the registrar's office at UC Santa Barbara.

The book bag was heavy and he was breathing hard by the time he reached the desk. He hoped the kid had the decency to be grateful that he'd come back all this way.

'Can I help you?' A pretty, blonde-haired woman looked up from her typing.

'Well, I hope so,' Willard said, heaving

the bag up onto the Formica counter. 'I think this belongs to a student of yours. He left it in my car.'

'I see,' she said, unzipping the bag. 'Well, I'm sure he'll be glad to get it back.'

'I'd have brought it back sooner, but I was out on the road. I'm a salesman. Cooper Electronics. Miller's the name. Willard Miller. Pacific Southwestern Division.'

'Well, it was nice of you to bring it back at all, Mr Miller. These kids can be so darned irresponsible.'

Willard shrugged. 'He was in a hurry. His father had just had a heart attack. He needed to get to L.A right away. I was headed there on my route.'

The woman opened a fat textbook and read the name inside, then punched up something on a computer and turned back to Willard.

'He's up in Hillward Hall, Mr Miller. Would you like me to see if he's in the dorm?'

'Well, no need, unless—yeah, what the heck. As long as I'm here, why not? Might as well find out what happened with his father. Seemed like a nice enough kid.'

She smiled pleasantly and he took a seat while the woman made the call.

'You're in luck,' she told him. 'He was

in the dorm and my, did he sound happy! He asked if you'd mind waiting just a few minutes. He'll be down here as soon as he can.'

The boy who walked in ten minutes later was six feet tall and black. Willard stared as he headed for the book bag and began to rummage through it.

'It's mine, all right.' He turned to Willard. 'You the guy who brought it back?' He held out his hand. 'Terence Mackey. Man, I can't thank you enough!'

Willard blinked. 'That's your book bag?'

Mackey grinned. 'Sure is! There's three hundred bucks' worth of books in that bag, plus my term paper notes.'

'But I—'

'Some dude stole it the other day while I was at the library. I've been bugging the police about it every day since. How'd you get ahold of it?'

'I gave a kid a ride. Picked him up out on the highway. He left the bag in the back of my car when I dropped him off in L.A.'

Mackey's eyes narrowed. 'Blond guy? Skinny?'

'Yeah, I guess he was.'

'That's the dude who stole it. I saw him grab it and take off out of the library. I ran after him, but I guess I wasn't fast enough. Sucker ran like a pro. Anyway, thanks for bringing it back. Oh, I offered a reward.'

The boy started to reach for his wallet, but Willard motioned him off. 'No, no, you keep it. I don't want your money. But I'd like to get my hands on that kid.'

Mackey smiled. 'Makes two of us, man. I'd like to get my hands on him, too.'

CHAPTER 4

Margie was making some notes on the Walters case when Mack buzzed her in her office.

'Police officer to see you,' he said. 'Sheriff's Lieutenant Paul Sellers.'

She did not recognize the lieutenant's name from any of the arrest reports she was working with.

'Thanks, Mack,' she said, putting aside the folder. 'Send him in, okay?'

The man who appeared in her doorway moments later was tall and solidly built, with an unruly thatch of dark hair and a pleasant if undistinguished face.

'Mrs Reed?' he asked. 'Lieutenant Paul Sellers. Glad to meet you, ma'am.'

Margie stood and extended a hand. 'It's Miss, Lieutenant, not Mrs.'

'Sorry.' The lieutenant waved a hand.

'The guard outside said—'

'I know.' Margie smiled. 'It's a small deception, mostly, I guess, because I deal with prisoners. Someone higher up decided somewhere along the way that if we're *missus*, we're somehow less vulnerable.'

Sellers raised an eyebrow. 'I see. Does it work?'

'I'm not sure.' Margie smiled. 'On the other hand, maybe it does. I've never had a prisoner propose marriage.'

The lieutenant smiled for the first time.

'Come on in,' she said. 'Have a seat.'

'I'm here about the call you made to sheriff's headquarters this morning.' He settled into the chair by her desk. He must have noticed her blank look. 'You called in to report a disturbance.'

'Oh, yes.' Margie touched a hand to her head. 'I'm sorry. Of course I did, yes. But the desk sergeant said—never mind. I thought you were here about a patient.'

'I see.' Sellers's expression was unreadable. 'I guess that's a natural assumption, but no, I'm not. It's about your call. I thought I'd ask you a few questions.'

Something in his manner made Margie uneasy. She had dealt with a lot of cops. It was clear to her that Lieutenant Paul Sellers had something serious on his mind.

'You told the desk sergeant you heard a noise in your apartment about twelve twenty this morning.'

'Yes,' Margie said, a queasy feeling settling in the pit of her stomach. 'Actually, it wasn't *in* my apartment. It was outside, somewhere. It woke me up. I thought at first it was a woman screaming—a short, sort of high pitched yell. But it was over so quickly that I began to wonder if maybe I'd been dreaming, or that maybe what I'd heard was an ambulance siren. I live not far from the hospital.'

The lieutenant nodded. 'Were you alone at the time? I mean, did anyone else hear it, too?'

'No, Lieutenant. I live alone. There was no one else in my apartment.'

'Then what happened?'

'Well, I listened for a minute. I guess I was a little disoriented. Although I didn't hear anything, I got out of bed and I went out into the corridor. I looked around, but there was no one out there.'

'You didn't see or hear anything?'

Margie shook her head. 'I went back inside and looked out the window. My bedroom window looks out over the courtyard. But I didn't see anything out there, either. I thought then about calling the police, but I guess I convinced myself I had imagined the whole thing or dreamed it, because everything seemed so—normal. And then my phone rang. It scared me, but it was my brother calling, with some rather disturbing news...I was distracted...' Her voice trailed off. 'Anyway, I didn't make the call.'

The lieutenant looked at her. 'But you called this morning. Why did you decide to do that?'

'Because, Lieutenant'—her voice was firmer—'I couldn't get it out of my mind. The more I thought about it, the more I believed that what I had heard was a scream.' She met the lieutenant's gaze directly. 'Something happened, didn't it?'

Sellers paused. 'I'm afraid so, yes. One of your neighbours was murdered. A flight attendant named Jeanne Kerns. Her roommate found the body this morning. It happened in the corner unit, the one next to yours.'

Tears sprang to Margie's eyes. For a moment she couldn't speak. 'How...?' she asked.

'Her skull was crushed, we think probably with a heavy glass vase.'

Margie brought her hands to her face. 'Oh, God...and I didn't call.'

Sellers was quiet while Margie collected herself. When he spoke, his voice was gentle. 'No reason for you to feel guilty, Miss Reed. My impression is, it happened very quickly. It isn't likely anyone could have gotten over there between the time

53

you heard the scream and the time she was killed.'

Margie nodded. 'I suppose you're right. But I feel so irresponsible. If I *had* called you might have had someone in the area by the time the attacker left.'

'Maybe,' Sellers said. 'That's one reason I wanted to talk to you now. We'd be grateful if you could try to bring to mind every detail of what you saw or heard last night. Also, I wondered if you have any knowledge about the comings and goings in that apartment.'

'Believe me, Lieutenant, I am trying to remember, but nothing comes to mind. I'm embarrassed to admit I never knew my next-door neighbour's name. I think I may have seen her once. She was a dark-haired woman about my age—'

The lieutenant shook his head. 'That would be the roommate. The victim had long, blonde hair.'

Margie frowned. 'Then I never saw her. At least I don't recall that I did.'

'What about visitors? Do you recall seeing other people going in or out of that apartment?'

Again she shook her head. 'I'm really sorry. Not that I remember.'

Sellers stood up, a gentle expression softening the planes of his face. 'Well, thanks for talking to me. And don't be too hard on yourself. Sometimes we remember things later. If you do think of anything, I'd appreciate a call. Let me give you a number.'

Margie watched him remove a card case from the left breast pocket of his coat. 'One more thing,' he said, handing her a card and looking directly at her. 'In all likelihood, Jeanne Kerns was killed by someone she'd admitted to her apartment—someone she knew rather than someone who surprised her, or forced his way in. But we can't be sure, not at this point, anyway, so don't take any chances. Keep your door locked at all times. Try to be alert to strangers.'

Despite herself, a little shiver snaked its way down Margie's spine. 'I will,' she said, smiling uncertainly as she rose to show him down the hall. 'Thanks. I promise I will call if anything else comes to mind.'

The lieutenant paused halfway to the front desk and looked back over his shoulder. 'So you work with prisoners.'

'Yes,' she said. 'I'm a forensic psychologist for the state.'

Sellers smiled. 'Interesting work, seeing inside the criminal mind. It's what every cop would like to do, get inside the heads of his suspects. So, tell me, is the jail full?'

'I think so at the moment, yes.'

'How many cases are yours?'

'Three,' Margie said. 'Two sex offenders and a felony animal torture.'

Sellers looked at her. 'Wouldn't be the Walters kid?'

She nodded.

'He's a weirdo, that one.'

Margie blinked. 'You know the case?'

'Actually, I've met the kid. He was working as a box boy three, four months ago at Gelson's on the boulevard. You know it? Anyway, the butcher found him in the meat locker one day, stabbing sides of beef with an ice pick. He yelled at him, and the kid turned around and brandished the ice pick at him.'

Margie frowned.

'The kid didn't hurt him—just stood there, staring at him, I guess. The butcher ran out, yelled for the manager, and the manager called the station. I took the call from the dispatcher because I happened to be in the neighbourhood. When I got there, Walters was cool as a cucumber. Like it was no big deal.'

It was the same reaction Margie had seen in Glenn. 'What happened then?' she asked.

'The manager fired the kid on the spot, and that was the end of that. Nobody pressed charges and I'm not certain that they would have stuck if they had. Anyway, the manager's name is Fred Weitz. You can talk to him, if you want to.'

'I will.' Margie nodded. 'I just got the case. I've only seen Walters once. The judge wants reports on competence for trial and criminal responsibility. I haven't even talked to the family yet, never mind his employers. But thanks, of course I'll check it out. I try to do a thorough work-up.'

Paul Sellers looked at her for a long moment. 'I'm sure you do,' he said.

Margie wondered why she'd thought at first that his face was undistinguished. He had wonderful eyes, clear and deep and the warmest shade of brown.

Terrence Mackey tossed the book bag on his bed and began to go through its contents: chemistry book, world lit, calculus, all there, and his dog-eared Roget's *Thesaurus*. His notebooks, programme card, all of it was there, even an old campus newspaper.

Terrence shook his head. The textbooks alone were worth a lot of bucks. The slimebag who stole it must not be a student, or he would have known that, too. He could have sold them back to the campus store and pocketed a tidy little sum.

No, the dude was no student, Terrence decided. The slimebag never wanted the bag, except as a cover to make him *look* like a student so he could hitch a ride to L.A.

It occurred to Terrence that he should call the police detective who took the report on the stolen bag, if only to tell him that he'd gotten it back after all, no thanks to Santa Barbara P.D.

What the hell, the cop didn't give a damn, and he had the bag back, anyway. That was the important thing, though Terrence had to admit he would have liked to see the slimebag hang.

He rooted around in the bottom of the bag for his combination lock. When he didn't find it, he checked one side pocket, then unzipped the other.

'Well, what do you know?' he muttered to himself. 'Looka, looka here...'

CHAPTER 5

Margie could feel her headache coming back. Glancing at her watch, she was surprised to realize that she had not taken time for lunch.

She had made a list of things to do with regard to the Walters case, and one by one she had checked them off in a neat, round hand, setting interview appointments, requesting files, and gathering assessment materials.

Now she was hungry enough that even the thought of cafeteria food was not enough to deter her. Getting up to stretch, she smoothed her skirt and reached for her linen jacket.

As she put it on, she stood at the window and looked out over the landscape, a patchwork of tract homes set into the hills, bisected by a near-deserted freeway.

Soon the afternoon sun would shift, casting long shadows on the yellowing hills, and Margie would have to confront the fact that she had to go home—alone. Home, where only hours before, a woman had been brutally murdered by an unknown assailant in a sprawling apartment complex peopled with uncaring strangers.

It was a fact she had steadfastly refused to think about as she clung to the day's routine, and one that now sent a wave of apprehension rippling through her body.

She had promised Lieutenant Sellers that she would rack her brain to remember something that might help, but in fact, she knew, she had kept herself busy enough so that she would not have to think at all. Even psychologists were good at playing mind games, sometimes better than most.

She took a yellow legal pad from her

desk and tucked it under her arm. Over lunch, she would make some notes about anything she could remember.

The cafeteria was nearly empty at this hour of the afternoon. Margie selected a wilting tuna salad and a large glass of iced tea and took them to a window table, balancing her note pad on the tray.

She picked at her lunch without appetite, chewing on soda crackers and sipping her tea as she thought about the night before.

She was convinced now that the scream had been real. She had heard it and it had awakened her, leaving her shaken, her heart pounding, as she'd turned to look at the clock. What had possessed her to go running into the hall was still something of a mystery, but she remembered her relief at seeing nothing and no one, and heading back to her apartment.

'Margie? Hey, are you all right?'

Margie looked up blankly. It was a moment before she fully recognized Chet Anderson's concerned face.

The psychologist pushed his glasses up and sat across from her. 'You look like you're a million miles away. What's the matter? The Walters case?'

Margie shook her head. 'No, Chet, it's something else. Something happened late last night and I guess I'm—just beginning to come to grips with it.'

Chet's obvious concern was comforting and in a matter of moments, though she had not intended to, Margie blurted out the whole story. She told him about the scream that woke her, her indecision about calling the police, her shock at learning that her next-door neighbour had been cruelly bludgeoned to death.

'My God, Margie!' Chet reached for her hand. 'I don't know what to say. Except there isn't a way in the world you're going home alone tonight.'

'Please, Chet.' Margie pulled her hand away to sweep up cracker crumbs with her napkin. 'I'm a big girl and I'm quite sure the police will be patrolling. I only told you because—I don't know—I guess I feel somehow responsible...'

'Responsible! How could you feel responsible? That police lieutenant was right. There was no way you could have done anything to prevent that murder from happening. By the time you heard that woman scream, it was already too late.'

'I know that.' Margie threw the napkin on her plate. 'Oh, God, Chet, I don't know. I deal with murderers all the time. You'd think I could handle this.'

Chet reached for her hand again, and this time she let him hold it. 'Listen,' he said. 'We deal with murderers, but rarely in our own backyards. You have every right to be angry and revolted and—yes, Margie, even scared.'

Margie felt hot tears spring to her eyes. She fought to keep them from spilling over. Chet's voice was quiet but confident, and she found herself listening closely.

'I meant what I said about your not going home alone,' he told her, gently squeezing her hand. 'Whether you want me to or not, I'm going with you. I intend to stay the night.'

She started to protest, but Chet would have none of it. 'Please, let me be a friend. I can sleep on the couch. Whatever you want. I just don't want you to be alone.'

Margie nodded. 'Thank you, Chet. It isn't necessary, but—'

'Settled. You finish your lunch. I'm going to make a few calls and go home to get a change of clothes. I'll be back by five. I'll come up to the office, and we'll go on together from there.'

She watched him go, his back straight, striding purposefully across the room. Then she took a pencil out of her purse and turned her attention to the legal pad.

Corridor empty, she began to write. *Looked down into empty stairwell. Went back into apartment.* No. Wait. That wasn't right. Margie paused, dropping the pencil, as she remembered something else—a fragmented image she had tried to suppress as she

62

tossed through the endless night, and which now sent a clutch of white-hot fear coursing through her stomach.

Some impulse had caused her to look up just as she entered her apartment. It was a sense, more than anything, that she was not alone, that someone was out there on the landing.

Margie could feel her heart beating through the thin voile of her blouse. She put down her glass and put her hands to her mouth as she realized what she had not wanted to face:

She had seen no one in the corridor last night. *But someone had seen her.*

It was cool and cloudy in Santa Barbara when Police Detective Ray Nance parked his unmarked Ford at the station. The weather suited his mood, he thought, pocketing his keys as he strode through the outer office.

His shoulder hurt from the punishing workout he'd given it on the tennis court at lunch, and Susie was still on him about buying a house when they hadn't even set a date for the wedding. But more than that, he was bugged as hell over his lack of progress on the Garcia case.

Why he had taken such an interest in the gardener's murder was a question he found hard to answer. It seemed to be a random killing by some faceless punk who had needed a few bucks for a snort. A very few bucks, in this case, Nance thought. The guy rarely carried more than ten or fifteen bucks, Garcia's wife had told him, and no jewellery but a little silver cross.

Maybe it was the wife who had gotten to him, with her stoic determination not to cry—that little bitty big-eyed waif in a huge, pregnant body, who had answered Nance's questions with perfect trust that he would learn who had murdered her husband.

'He have faith in God, my Ramon,' she had told him. 'He wear all the time, he never take off this little silver cross around his neck.'

She described the filigreed crucifix Garcia had worn, made of cheap Mexican silver, the little cross that was nowhere in evidence when the gardener's body was found.

She had looked down at her huge belly, her voice barely a whisper. 'I don't know why God let this happen to Ramon. Is hard for me to have faith.'

Then she'd looked up again at Nance, her eyes wide and glistening. 'You will find him, Detective Nance. You find my husband's killer. You bring me back Ramon's crucifix. Maybe then I have faith, too...'

But he had not found Garcia's killer, and he was realistic enough to know that time was running out and it would not be much longer before the gardener's murder, like the gardener himself, faded into obscurity.

It was twenty minutes to three when Emma Danziger finished checking medications. In twenty minutes she would be off shift. God, how she wanted to get her shoes off.

She locked the cabinet, picked up the charts, and dropped them on her supervisor's desk. Then she rubbed her sore foot, groaned aloud, and set off down the hall for final bed check.

If there was ever a time when the floor was calm, this was likely to be it. It was after lunch, and still a while till dinner; the flow of visitors would not pick up again until sometime in the early evening. Most patients were back on the ward from surgery or treatments and were happy to sleep away the afternoon.

It made the routine patient count easier, and Emma breezed right along, hobbling a little but moving as purposefully as her blistered foot would allow.

She paused in the doorway of 6114. All the beds were full. A television was on, but it seemed to Emma that all five patients were dozing.

She moved closer to the foot of the bed that had been empty when she'd gone to lunch. It was now occupied by a youngish fellow with an acned face, dishwater-blond hair, and a scraggly growth of beard.

A chart had been hung at the foot of his bed. Emma stepped closer to read it. The patient had been sent up from the emergency room at ten thirty this morning, complaining of stomach pain, and was reassigned here to bed 6114E. So where had he been at eleven thirty, when Emma went to lunch?

Overcome with a feeling that the patient was watching her, Emma shifted her glance to his face. His eyes were closed and he was breathing deeply, arms straight down at his sides.

Emma looked at him, frowning slightly. This one was going to bear watching. She read the name at the top of the chart. Kiefer. Dennis Kiefer.

CHAPTER 6

Paco's Mexiburgers, Paul Sellers thought, stretching his legs out in front of him on the park bench, were highly overrated in his book.

The lieutenant finished a last big bite, washed it down with a swig of Pepsi, and promised himself he would take no more recommendations about food from the guys at Station Two.

He had been in the neighbourhood, having spent twenty minutes with the bartender at Sidney's, and since the likelihood of a decent dinner was beginning to seem remote, he'd decided to stop for the take-out special on his way back to the station.

He should have stuck to frozen yogurt, or a salad from Mickey D's. On the other hand, he thought, getting up to find a wastebasket, he had needed this respite in the park.

It was a clear and golden afternoon, swept clean by last night's winds. Even the trees seemed fuller and greener, as though the dust had been shaken from their limbs. Behind a chain link fence not far from where he stood, some kids were playing flag football. Sellers wandered over, his hands stuffed into his pockets, and stopped to watch.

Jamie would have been eight this month. Old enough for football. Sellers's mouth tightened. Why did everything seem to come down to what might have been?

He turned slowly and ambled back to where he'd parked his car. There wasn't time for self-indulgence. He had plenty of work to do.

Jeanne Kerns's body had been taken for autopsy. The forensics team was at work. Tomorrow he would take the roommate back to the apartment to see what else was missing. She had already noted that an opal ring was gone from the victim's finger—a birthstone ring Kerns wore all the time on the fourth finger of her right hand.

Outwardly there were no signs that the apartment had been ransacked. However, if Jeanne Kerns had known her killer, robbery was not the prime motive. Sellers would not speculate further until the lab reports were in.

The bartender at Sidney's had told him Kerns was a regular, as were a number of flight attendants. He thought he remembered seeing her last night, but he didn't know when she'd left, and if she had been with someone in particular, he wasn't able to say. He was shocked to learn that Kerns had been killed, and he promised to question the regulars, but Sellers planned to go back himself to talk to the late-night crowd.

It was well past four when he got to his desk and scanned a fistful of messages, among them one from Margie Reed, the psychologist he'd seen earlier.

He liked Reed. She was bright, confident, and obviously independent, but sensitive enough to be moved to tears over the death of a perfect stranger.

She'd been shaken, too, maybe too upset to have been much help to him this morning. He got himself some coffee from a vending machine and dialled her number at the hospital.

'This is Margie Reed.'

'Paul Sellers, Miss Reed. I just got back to the office.'

'Oh, thank you for calling. I've been thinking, and a couple of things have come to mind. Nothing major, but if you have some time, maybe we could talk again.'

'Happy to,' Sellers sipped his coffee. 'How late do you stay at the hospital?'

'About five,' she said.

'Are you going straight home?'

He heard her pause. 'I am.'

'Suppose I meet you there? I was going to go by anyway, talk to some of your neighbours. About five fifteen?'

'That sounds fine.'

'Good. I'll see you then.'

Sellers brought the coffee up to his lips and thought about Margie Reed. *Miss* Margie Reed, he reminded himself. Miss Margie Reed...not Mrs.

Detective Ray Nance was getting ready to go home when he heard Terrence Mackey in the outer office. That was all he needed, another go-round about a stolen university book bag.

He was about to call the desk to say he was gone for the day, when the kid appeared in his doorway, with a satisfied grin on his broad face and a book bag over his shoulder.

'Detective Nance, busy cop, I presume.' The kid slipped the bag off his shoulder.

'Good for you, you got your bag back. Or did you have to pop for a new one?'

'I got it back, no thanks to you. A guy brought it back from L.A, where it went with the slimebag who ripped it off so he could hitch himself a ride.'

The detective nodded. 'Look, Mackey, I'm glad you got it back. I did what I could, but you have to understand this was just not priority stuff—'

'Uh-huh,' Mackey said. 'So now that I've got it back, you'd just as soon forget about it.'

'What should I do? Maybe dust it for prints? It's porous, I can't do that.'

'Well, I got something better than prints, if you even want to *try* to find the sucker who ripped it off.'

Nance sighed. 'Okay, Mackey. Let's just cut to the chase. Why don't you show me what you've got and then we'll go from there?'

The kid made an elaborate show of heaving the bag on the desk. He unzipped a pocket and pulled out what looked to Nance like a green nylon jacket.

'That's it?' Nance asked. 'A nylon windbreaker. Now you'll tell me it isn't yours.'

'Right,' said Mackey. 'It isn't mine. So it must belong to the thief.'

'Good,' Nance said. 'Did you check the pockets? Maybe he left us a business card.'

'As a matter of fact—' Mackey grinned, reaching into a pocket.

He pulled out a card. Nance read it out loud. 'Joseph Landesmann, M.D Physician and surgeon, Vejar State Hospital, Santa Barbara, California. Well, you'll pardon my scepticism, but it isn't likely the doctor ripped off your bag.'

'There's something written on the back,' Mackey said. 'Maybe he'll remember who he gave it to. Oh, yeah, and this.'

He reached back into the pocket and brought out something else. He tossed it casually on Nance's desk.

It was a little silver cross.

Chet Anderson was in Margie's office at three minutes to five. 'Whew. It's warm out there.' He took off his glasses and smoothed back his shaggy blond hair. 'How're you doing?'

'I'm fine,' Margie said.

'Well, good. Let's go, then.'

She let him help her on with her jacket. 'Listen, Chet, I'm not so sure...I really appreciate what you're trying to do, but really, I'll be fine.'

'Nothing doing.' Chet was firm. 'You're not going home alone. I'll sleep better on your couch, knowing you're okay, than I would in my own bed at home.'

Margie started to say something, but Chet would not let her. 'Friends, Margie. Friends. I'd like to think that if I needed help, you'd be there for me, too.'

There was no point in arguing, Margie saw, picking up her purse. It was sweet of Chet to worry. Maybe she *would* rest easier with someone else in the apartment.

They took the elevator down eleven floors and went out the main entrance, traversing the parking lot to the sheltered area where both their cars were parked.

'Why don't you leave yours here?' Chet asked. 'We'll be coming back together in the morning.'

But Margie said she'd feel better driving her own car. 'Having a POSSLQ around is one thing,' she smiled. 'Don't ask me to give up my wheels.'

'Person of the Opposite Sex Sharing Living Quarters. I like it.' Chet grinned back at her. 'It has a certain ring. We might even learn to like the arrangement. Look at all the money we'd save.'

Margie settled herself in the Honda. 'I've got bad news for you. I snore,' she joked. 'You remember where I live, at the Wentworth Apartments, on Wentworth and Second. It's just a couple of miles down the road.'

The winds were gone, a grey-brown shroud already settling on the horizon, and Margie could feel the Santa Ana heat radiating through her windshield. She turned on the air conditioning, crossed the parking lot, and turned left toward home, making a conscious effort to confine her thoughts to what she might find in her refrigerator.

She'd been trying to eat more healthfully of late. There was probably some yogurt and salad makings. Well, if that wasn't enough to satisfy Chet, they could always order a pizza. The thought was comforting. She deserved a pizza. It had been a difficult day.

She began to hope she'd find a message on her machine from Rob, telling her everything was okay, that Trisha was home and everything was fine. It would be one less thing for her to stew about. Then she turned left again into the apartment complex, glancing in her rearview mirror.

Chet was not behind her. He must have been stopped at a light. No doubt he'd be along in a minute. She pulled into her parking space as Lieutenant Sellers drove up from the other direction, waved at her, parked in a visitor space, and unfolded himself from his car.

'Good timing,' she said.

He saluted jauntily. 'Listen, I was thinking about some dinner. I'll be pulling a long shift tonight. If you're hungry, I thought we could talk over dinner and then I'd just go on about my work.'

Before Margie could respond, Chet drove up alongside them. 'Okay to park over here?'

'Yes, fine.' She could see the lieutenant's face cloud. 'I'm sorry,' she managed to say. 'This is a co-worker of mine, Chet Anderson,' she said as the blond psychologist joined them. 'Chet, this is Lieutenant Paul Sellers. He's investigating the murder.'

The men shook hands, mumbling pleasantries. Margie could feel her cheeks warming. For reasons not entirely clear, she felt she owed the lieutenant an explanation.

'Chet was worried about my spending the night alone,' she said. 'He offered to

74

stay...' Her voice trailed off.

But Sellers brushed it off. 'A good idea. That you not be alone, I mean.'

She wanted to thank him for the offer of dinner, but she felt it would make matters worse. 'Well,' she said, lifting her chin and leading the way to her building. 'Lieutenant, you already know where it is. Chet, it's just up here...'

She was halfway up the brick walkway when she noticed the figure in the doorway—a young blonde woman, sitting on the steps, with a baby asleep in her lap.

'Trisha!' She ran toward her sister-in-law. 'Oh, my God, it's Trisha!'

Trisha looked from one to the other of Margie's two companions. 'Hi, Marg,' she said in a small voice. 'I guess I should have called first, huh?'

CHAPTER 7

Margie cradled the baby in one arm as she unlocked her front door. 'Rebecca Marjorie,' she cooed. 'Oh, you are precious! Did you know you were named for your Auntie Margie!'

Trisha followed Margie in quickly,

carrying a small suitcase. 'She's wet, I'll bet. Hungry, too. Do you mind if I find the bedroom, Margie, so I can change her diaper and feed her?'

'Of course, Trisha. It's there on the right.' Margie set down her purse and keys and reluctantly handed her the baby. Then she turned back to the doorway, where the two men stood looking awkward.

The lieutenant spoke first. 'Maybe this is a bad time. I could come back later tonight.'

Margie shook her head. 'Come in, Lieutenant. I really do want to talk to you.'

Chet shrugged, his hands in his pockets. 'Looks like maybe you won't need me, after all.'

He looked so forlorn that Margie hesitated. 'I appreciate your offer to be here.'

'No problem,' Chet said. 'I'd be happy to stay if—'

'No, Chet, we'll be fine. But thanks again. You're a good friend.'

'Well, I guess I'll see you in the morning. You have my number, if you do need anything.'

Margie nodded. 'Thanks.'

She watched him go, then turned to Sellers, whose presence seemed to fill the small living room. 'Please, Lieutenant, won't you sit down? Can I get you something to drink?'

Sellers shook his head. 'Nothing, thanks. Are you sure you don't want me to come back later?'

'Let me just check on Trisha and the baby. I'll be right with you, I promise.'

Trisha was fastening Rebecca's diaper when Margie opened the door. 'Do you need anything?'

'No, thanks, Margie. I carry her main course with me.' Trisha began to unfasten her blouse and settle herself on the bed. 'You go out there and see to your guests. I'll be out in a little while.'

Margie closed the door behind her and rested against it for a moment. Of course Trisha thought the men were friends. Why would she think otherwise? Margie had introduced Sellers as a lieutenant, but that was simply an occupation. Trisha had no way of knowing that the lieutenant was here on business.

'Lieutenant,' she said, going back to the living room and sitting across from Sellers, 'tell me you think it's perfectly safe here. I mean, my sister-in-law and the baby...'

'I can't tell you it's perfectly safe, but I can tell you we'll be patrolling. You probably didn't notice, in your excitement over your sister-in-law, but there's an officer in the centre of the courtyard—and two others are posted in the complex. It's standard procedure at a crime scene.'

Margie nodded, shaken to admit that her home was now a crime scene and worried that Trisha and Rebecca had come to her for help and she couldn't guarantee their safety.

Sellers must have sensed her uneasiness. His voice was very gentle. 'Unfortunately, with a crime as sensational as this, it's impossible to keep it from the press. They were all over the place earlier today, and the story's been all over the airwaves. We'll keep a close watch to keep the curiosity seekers out as well as to protect the neighbourhood, although frankly the likelihood of the perpetrator coming back is usually pretty slim.'

'What if—' Margie cleared her throat. 'What if he thinks someone saw him?'

'The perpetrator?'

Margie nodded.

'You told me you didn't see anyone.'

'I know,' Margie said, her voice low. 'But I think he may have seen me.'

Sellers paused, then sat forward in his seat. 'Why don't you tell me what you mean?'

Margie described the eerie feeling that had come over her in the hall, the sixth sense that had made her look up into the empty landing.

'It's like that feeling you get,' she said, 'when you're driving your car and you sense another driver staring at you. You look over and he's embarrassed or something and his eyes are back on the road. That's as near as I can describe it, Lieutenant, a feeling that I was being watched. But by the time I looked up, there was no one there.'

Sellers seemed to be watching her closely. 'Is it possible you only imagined it?'

'Maybe,' Margie said. 'It would be very comforting to think I had just imagined it. But what if someone *was* there, and he managed to get out of sight just before I looked up?'

Sellers nodded. 'I'll have a look upstairs. There's probably an exit to the roof. You did tell me that when you came back inside, you went directly to the window.'

'Yes,' Margie said. 'But that's another thing. I went to the window twice—once when I came in, and I didn't see anything, and again after my brother called. It may not mean anything, but the second time I looked, I saw someone jogging toward the main road.'

'How much later would this have been?'

'Eight, maybe ten minutes later. I didn't think anything about it at the time since everybody out here jogs. Even late at night, after a shift at the hospital. A lot of hospital employees live here.'

Sellers took a notebook from his pocket. 'What can you tell me about the jogger?'

'Not much, I'm afraid. He was too far away. It was a man. Tallish. Thin. I'm sorry. It was dark. Even if I'd tried, I don't think I could have seen what he was wearing.'

'Mmm...' Sellers put the notebook away and rose slowly to his feet. 'Maybe someone else got a better look. I'll know more when I talk to your neighbours. I imagine most of them are home by now. I also want to look around upstairs.'

Margie got up and extended a hand. 'Thank you for coming, Lieutenant. I'll have to tell Trisha what happened, of course, but at least I know the area's being watched.'

Sellers's handshake was firm but gentle. 'You can bet on that, Miss Reed.'

'Margie,' she said. 'I like that better, away from the office, anyway.'

'Margie. That's nice. An old-fashioned name. Well. I'd better get to work.'

'You know, Lieutenant,' she said, walking him to the door, 'you never did have dinner.'

His smile was genuine. 'Occupational hazard. I'll pick up something later. As long as I'm here, I might as well finish up. I'll be an hour, anyway.'

'I have an idea,' Margie said. 'I have a

guest to feed, too. Suppose I have a pizza delivered. Would you care to come back and join us?'

He looked at her as if she'd invented the wheel. 'How can I turn that down?'

'Good. It's settled. Take as long as you need. It'll be here whenever you're ready.'

Margie closed the door after Paul Sellers and went to check on Trisha. She hoped that once Rebecca had been fed, Trisha might want to call home.

'Trisha...' She tapped on the bedroom door. 'Honey, it's me. Can I come in?' There was no answer. Margie turned the knob and quietly opened the door.

Trisha lay curled in the centre of the bed, her blouse and bra still undone. She looked not much older than a child herself with the blush of sleep on her cheeks. She was sleeping soundly, with her left arm curved protectively around the baby. Rebecca slept, too, her tiny mouth inches from her mother's breast, still making little sucking noises as though she were remembering her dinner.

Margie watched them with a rush of feeling she could not quite identify—love, protectiveness, sadness, longing, all bunched together in her chest.

It seemed impossible that nearly a year had passed since that night in the cabin in the Berkshires. There'd been so much to celebrate then—Trisha's pregnancy and Frank's announcement that he and Margie were engaged.

'I knew it! I told you, Rob, didn't I tell you?' Trisha had embraced them both.

Rob had beamed. 'I couldn't be happier. My big sister and my best friend!'

It was Margie who discovered that they'd left the grocery store without so much as a bottle of wine and Rob who insisted that a night like this deserved a champagne toast.

Trisha suggested they toast with cocoa, in the blue mugs she made for each of them. But Rob had already begun to pull on his boots. 'Come on, Frank. We'll be back in no time.'

'Something's wrong,' Margie said when they hadn't returned nearly an hour later.

Trisha's eyes had been wide with worry. 'Come on. We can walk to the store.'

They pulled on their boots and were fastening their parkas when they heard the reassuring crunch of tyres on snow. But instead of Frank and Rob, it was the grim face of a state trooper that loomed in the cabin doorway.

A robbery, he said. Something about a shooting. Even now, Margie's memory was blurred. All she heard clearly was that Frank was dead—slain by a penny-ante thief.

'My husband—' Trisha's face was drained of colour, her eyes enormous in her face.

He was fine. He was at the station. They would go there together. Margie could not remember the drive. Only Rob's pinched face, close to hers, sobbing, clinging to her and Trisha.

It seemed like hours before Margie emerged from the misty haze of her shock—long enough to absorb what had happened in the near-deserted mountain store.

A man had burst in suddenly, Rob told them, apparently unaware that he and Frank were browsing in the gourmet section. The man demanded money from the youthful clerk and shouted warnings to hurry.

Rob and Frank had exchanged glances, he said, and edged toward the front of the store expecting that, between the two of them, they could overpower the robber from behind.

'He must have seen us—or sensed us,' Rob sobbed. 'He just opened fire. He was crazy! He kept firing—rounds and rounds—he just—kept—shooting...'

Rob had been able to take cover, he told them. Somehow, miraculously, he'd survived. But when it was over—his voice hoarse—Frank and the clerk were dead. The robber fled. Rob called the troopers and waited in the shambles until they got there.

Margie squeezed her eyes shut, as if to block out the memory. Then she opened them to look again at Trisha and her sleeping child.

How beautiful they were, she thought. She watched them for a long moment. Then she quietly closed the door and left them to their dreams.

What in the world could possibly have happened to drive Rob and Trisha apart? Maybe she should call her brother, let him know they were here. No, she told herself. That was Trisha's place. She would be awake soon enough.

She picked up her purse and the set of keys she'd left lying on the hall table, and she fingered the funny little wooden doll that hung from the silver-coloured chain. It had been in Frank's pocket on the night he was killed, a tiny figure painted black, with white half-moons on its cheeks.

Margie shuddered, remembering how she'd felt when the trooper had given her Frank's 'effects.' Effects, she thought. What an ugly word for all that was left of someone's life. She'd sent most of them to Frank's mother in Boston, but she'd wanted something to keep, and she'd selected the funny little talisman and hung it from her key chain.

She hefted it now, the tiny memento that was all she had left of Frank. Then she tossed the key chain into her purse and headed for the kitchen.

She found the phone book in a lower cabinet and opened it up to the yellow pages. She had lost her taste for pizza, but Trisha would be hungry. And the lieutenant, too. She found the number and began to dial. A large pizza with everything...

Denny lay in his hospital bed, staring up at the ceiling. Tomorrow he'd find a way to get past that nosy nurse and go exploring in the hospital. For tonight, he would enjoy the crisp, white sheets and the firm pillow under his head.

Any hospital was a damn sight better than any homeless shelter Denny had ever crashed in. He stretched and yawned, remembering happily the first time he'd discovered that about hospitals.

It was in Coos Bay, up in Oregon. He'd been working in one of the lumber camps. It wasn't his fault he'd gotten hurt. It was a stupid freak accident. He remembered how surprised he had been when he woke up and found himself in a hospital, and how good it felt to be clean and warm and practically waited on by nurses.

A guy could get used to this, he remembered thinking. Even the food wasn't bad—a damned sight better than some he'd had in the ten years he'd been on his own.

Free bed. Free meals. Hot showers. Dry towels. No priests. No counsellors. No social workers. You could keep your mouth shut and nobody bugged you. That was what Denny liked best.

When his leg was healed, they shipped him out. But he hadn't gone back to the camp. He hocked the loot he'd snagged at the hospital and headed for the open road.

He got as far as Grant's Pass before he ran out of money, and he had to ice that jerk at the self-serve gas station who wouldn't open the till. He was moving fast by the time he heard cop sirens screaming back to the gas station, but he needed a place to hole up quick and that was when the bright idea occurred to him.

He slipped into a grocery store, bought some rat poison and managed to force down just enough to give himself a bellyache. Then he went to the county hospital and puked on the emergency room floor. Before he knew it, he'd

86

been admitted. Bam! Easy as pie. He was off the streets, safe and sound, until long after the cops had stopped looking.

From Grant's Pass, it had been a short haul across the state line to California. And except for the close call he'd had up at Vejar, the hospital gig was a snap. A little rat poison, or a taste of oleander, enough to make himself sick. He could get himself admitted anytime he wanted and he didn't even have to change his name. Denny smiled. Nobody checked. The system had a soft spot for transients.

Denny wished there were someone around who could appreciate how smart he was, how he managed to get himself safely off the streets where the cops would never look.

He'd been disappointed to find nothing but a twenty in the stewardess's eelskin wallet, especially since he knew he was taking a chance by snuffing her in her own apartment. But he'd managed to get the ring off her finger before he headed out. The ring would be worth a nice few bucks if he ever wanted to hock it.

All he had to do was bide his time and keep a lid on his temper. All he had to do was what he did best: ease on into the landscape...

CHAPTER 8

Paul Sellers let his coffee grow cold while he read the pathologist's report on Jeanne Kerns, scribbling notes that only he would be able to decipher later.

Cause of death, as he expected, was blood loss resulting from a blow to the head. It was a crushing blow, the lieutenant reflected, delivered with enough force to fracture the skull, pierce the dura mater, and reduce the brain to pulp.

Suspect is tall, Sellers scribbled on a yellow legal pad, *prob six feet or more.* Jeanne Kerns had been five feet nine inches in height. If, as he thought, she was assaulted while she was standing upright, her killer would have to be tall enough to deliver that kind of crushing blow.

There were no other bruises on the woman's body, no skin, blood, or fibre fragments under her fingernails, no signs of a physical struggle preceding the fatal blow. Neither was there semen in the vaginal tract or any indication that the victim had had sexual contact around the time of her death.

Sellers's pencil tapped a stippling of dots

across the surface of the yellow paper.

The victim's roommate told him Kerns was in the habit of bringing men home at night, and Sellers had talked to several guys at Sidney's last night who admitted to having been among them. No one at the bar could remember clearly if Kerns had left with anyone the night before. Whoever was with her, Sellers thought, apparently had not been thinking of romance.

Or if he had, then something had happened to make him change his mind.

Ck w/roommate, Sellers scrawled. *Victim carry a lot of cash?*

The lieutenant reached for his tepid coffee and drained it in a single swig. The forensics report, due later today, would probably confirm what he knew. The apartment showed no signs of forced entry. Kerns had either let her attacker in or had left the door unlocked and been surprised by an intruder.

He thought of Margie Reed, who'd locked the bolt on her door last night the minute he left her apartment, and he found it hard to believe that any woman today would ignore such a simple precaution. He added an entry under *Ck w/roommate: wd victim leave door unlocked?*

Sellers tossed the report aside and leaned back in his chair, remembering what Margie had told him last night about her near-encounter in the stairwell.

He had climbed the two flights to the topmost landing, but the entrance to the roof was locked. It was always locked, according to the manager, and Sellers found no evidence of tampering. Very likely, the killer had merely slipped out of Kerns's apartment, taken the stairs down, and walked away from the complex.

If that were the case, it was unlikely that Margie had been seen from an upper floor. So why was it she had the feeling that someone had been watching? And why was it that not another soul in the building had been aware of a disturbance?

Pushing his chair back, he stared morosely at the bare walls of his cubicle. Some of his cronies had lined their walls with photos or big, frondy plants. But Sellers had a brown thumb and nobody's photos to hang.

He had a crazy urge to call Margie. He could thank her for the pizza last night. He was looking at the phone when it rang shrilly.

'Homicide. Sellers speaking.'

'Lieutenant? This is Margie Reed. I hope I'm not disturbing you. I wanted to thank you for being there last night and for helping me explain it all to Trisha.'

Sellers sat forward. 'No problem,' he said. 'I was just about to call you. The pizza was great. Thanks for inviting me. I guess I never would have had dinner.'

'I'm sorry,' she said. 'I kept you too long.'

'No, really. Not at all.'

He heard her pause. 'I guess I was more upset than I was willing to admit at first. I have to tell you it was kind of reassuring, having a cop eating pizza in my living room.'

He wanted to tell her he would volunteer for duty for as long as she wanted him around. Instead he said, 'Well, we can do it again. I'll even bring a bottle of wine.'

She laughed. 'You're getting ahead of me, Lieutenant. Actually, I was thinking about Sunday. I'm a decent cook when I get the chance, and I'm planning an honest-to-goodness dinner. If you're free, or if there's someone you want to bring—'

'There's no one,' he said, too quickly. 'If that's an invitation, I accept. But there is one thing.'

'What's that?' she asked.

'Can I leave the lieutenant at home?'

She paused for a second, then laughed again. 'Of course. We'll expect you at five.'

Margie was still smiling when she put down the phone. It would be fun to cook a big dinner and have people around to share it with. And, she had to admit, she was beginning to like Paul Sellers.

Her smile faded as she realized wistfully that she wished her brother were here. She missed him terribly, and it set her to thinking about what was going on between him and Trisha. Tonight, at least, she would talk to her sister-in-law. But now she had plenty to do.

She read and initialled the transcript of a report that was due in court tomorrow, glad for the opportunity to focus her attention entirely on her work. She was assembling the testing materials she would need later for her session with Glenn Walters when Mack buzzed her to let her know that Walters's parents had arrived.

'Good morning,' she said, ushering them in. 'Thank you both for coming. My name is Margie Reed and, as I told you on the phone, I'm a psychologist who will be working with Glenn.'

John Walters preceded his wife into the small office. He was a big man, fiftyish, Margie guessed, with the ruddy face and rheumy eyes of a man who drank too much. Wordlessly he selected the larger of two chairs and sat without invitation, while Beatrice Walters hovered in the doorway, fussing with the straps of her purse.

'Is that where Glenn is?' the woman asked, looking back over her shoulder.

'Yes,' Margie said. 'To your left, down the hall. Past the double doors. I'm afraid it won't be possible for you to see him today, but—'

'No, no, that's all right. He's locked up, isn't he? Yes, of course, he would be...'

The small, birdlike woman came into the room and slipped into the available chair. She tugged at the skirt of her white nylon uniform and set her purse squarely in her lap.

Margie noted the ill-fitting uniform and Walters's oil-stained jeans. They were strange trappings for a couple who hailed from the wealthy resort town of Scottsdale and who, apparently, could afford an expensive attorney to represent their son in court.

'Are you a nurse, Mrs Walters?' Margie asked, taking her seat across from them.

Glenn's mother smiled wanly. 'Oh, no. No, I'm a waitress.' She glanced down at the watch on her wrist. 'I work at Joyce's Coffee Shop. And I hope you don't mind, but I don't have much time. I told them I'd be there for the lunch rush.'

'Well,' Margie said, 'I appreciate your coming, and I promise not to keep you too long. Basically, what I'd like is some family history to help me understand Glenn better.'

Mrs Walters sighed audibly and looked

down at her purse. 'I guess I can save us both some time. I had Glenn in Payson, Arizona, when I was just past seventeen. He had no daddy till I married John when Glenn was six years old. He never was adopted legally, but he always used John's name.'

From the rapid monotone of the recitation, Margie guessed that Mrs Walters had given this speech before, perhaps many times, to the series of 'shrinks' that Glenn had already alluded to.

'What was Glenn like when he was six, Mrs Walters?'

The woman shrugged. 'Just a boy. No different than most of the boys his age. Always tearin' around.'

'How did he react to suddenly having a father?' Margie looked directly at Walters.

Walters glanced quickly over at his wife. 'Okay, I guess,' he said.

Mrs Walters kept her eyes down. 'John tried to be a good father. We never had any other kids. Glenn was all we had.'

Margie waited, but neither of the Walterses added anything more. 'What do you do for a living, Mr Walters?'

Again, the man glanced at his wife. 'Retired, you could say. Worked the Gila County copper mines up until I had my accident. Broke both legs, got hurt pretty bad. Ain't been able to work much since.'

'Is that when you moved to Scottsdale?' Margie asked.

'Yep,' Walters nodded. 'Six years ago. Had a mighty fine house. Right nice.'

Margie smiled. 'I'm sure it was. I've heard Scottsdale is lovely.'

Mrs Walters raised her head and looked for the first time at Margie. 'Expensive, too. I'm sure you've heard that. You're wondering how we could afford it. Well, we got a settlement after—the accident. We went to Scottsdale for Glenn. I thought if things were nicer for him, he might settle down and make friends.'

Margie smiled at Mrs Walters. 'And how did that work out? Glenn would have been about twelve years old. What did he think about the move?'

The woman looked down at her lap again. 'Didn't seem to make no difference. Glenn wasn't ever much interested in friends. He mostly kept to himself.'

'How did he do in school, Mrs Walters?'

'Fair. I guess he did fair.'

'Was he ever in trouble with the police?' Margie asked.

Mrs Walters looked pointedly at her watch. 'I'm sorry,' she said. 'We really have to leave. I have to be at the restaurant by eleven. Jobs aren't easy to come by, you know. I can't afford to lose this one.'

Margie wondered what had happened

to the fine house in Scottsdale, why the family had moved again, and how they felt about Glenn's arrest. But it was clear the Walterses were not inclined to talk anymore today, and there were other sources Margie could tap before she spoke to them again.

'Well,' she said, 'I appreciate your coming. I'm sure we'll talk some more. Meanwhile, if I can answer anything for you, please feel free to ask.'

The couple seemed to rise in a single motion, as though they'd been freed from bondage, Mr Walters, for all of his bulk, moving as swiftly as his wife.

'Thank you, no,' Glenn's mother said. 'We'll be talking to Glenn's new lawyer.'

In short order they were out of the office, moving down the hall. They did not look back as they waited for Mack to release the outer door.

Appearances could be deceiving, Margie realized, watching their hasty exit. But John Walters did not move like a man who was permanently disabled. At her desk, she picked up Glenn's file and found her notes on Arizona. To her request for juvenile records, she added, *background check: J.W.*

In Santa Barbara, Detective Ray Nance scrunched up his left shoulder and listened

96

to Susie on the telephone while he went through his notes on the Garcia case.

'It's a darling house, Ray,' Susie was saying. 'A fixer-upper, but with all kinds of potential. A little paint, some wallpaper, you know. The place could be really cute.'

Nance saw that his last call to Landesmann had been nearly an hour ago. The doctor's conference should be over by now. He could get a call any minute.

'Well, it sounds good, Soos,' he told his fiancée. 'I'll try to take a look at it Saturday.'

'Saturday may well be too late,' Susie said. 'The price is right, it's going to get snapped up. And Ray, the people want out by Christmas. We talked about a Christmas wedding.'

Nance wondered for the hundredth time why he couldn't seem to make the commitment. He loved Susie. He wanted to marry her. Why wouldn't he set a date?

He heard two short beeps on his end of the line. He had another call waiting. 'Listen, Soos, can we talk about it tonight? I've got a call waiting I want to take.'

Susie sighed. 'Okay, Ray. I'll see you later. Bye-bye.'

He heard the line go dead, hung up briefly, and picked up on the first ring.

'Detectives. Ray Nance.'

'Hold a minute, can you, Detective? Dr Landesmann will be right with you.'

The doctor's voice sounded brusque, hurried. 'This is Dr Landesmann. You called me?'

'Yes, Doctor. I'm investigating the murder of a gardener that took place on the grounds of the hospital a week ago today. Ramon Garcia. You must have heard about it.'

'Yes, yes. I recall. What can I do for you, Detective? There are five interns waiting for me on rounds.'

'Sir, a silver cross was taken from the gardener's body, presumably by the assailant. The cross was found in the pocket of a jacket that a hitchhiker left in L.A. Also in the pocket was one of your cards. The hitchhiker may have been a patient.'

The doctor hesitated. 'Detective Nance, I see hundreds of patients in this hospital. Undoubtedly dozens of them leave here every week with one of my cards in their possession.'

'Yes, sir,' Nance said. 'But I'm hoping you may be able to narrow that number somewhat. There's a note written on the back of the card with an address that turns out to be the Salvation Army Shelter here in Santa Barbara. If you check your records for September twenty-third, maybe you can remember who you gave it to.'

'Mmm,' the doctor said. 'I don't know. I can try, but it may take me a while to get to it. We see a lot of patients, a surprising number of transients. There's a damned lot of paper work attached.'

'I'm sure there is,' Nance told him. 'But we'd appreciate your giving it a shot. September twenty-third. Maybe a patient you discharged, who asked you for the address of a shelter. I've asked Medical Records for a list of discharges that day, but it would help if you could come up with a name.'

'Mmm,' the doctor said again. 'All right, I'll try to get to it. I have your number. If I come up with anything, I'll certainly give you a call.'

'Thank you, sir. I'll expect to hear from you—' Nance heard the line go dead.

The detective opened the top drawer of his desk and pulled out a square white envelope. In it was the gardener's silver cross, recently back from the lab. It had been dusted for prints, but anything viable checked out to the kid, Terrence Mackey, who'd handled it any number of times before he'd brought it to the station.

Nance traced the shape of it through the envelope and thought about the gardener's wife. It would not be enough to give her back the cross. He wanted to give her Ramon's killer.

He found himself wondering if Susie would grieve for him the way Rosie Garcia grieved for her husband. He knew she would, and he felt ashamed for even considering the question.

Then it occurred to him, in a crazy instant, why he had been putting Susie off. A policeman's wife. Always poised for the worst. That's what he was asking her to be.

But then, the gardener's wife had had every reason to expect her husband home that night he was killed. If life was fragile, it was fragile for everyone. Nance could testify to that.

The detective hefted the little white envelope. Tonight he and Susie would set the date.

CHAPTER 9

The deserted twelfth floor of Santa Clarita State Hospital was more than Denny could have hoped for.

He had planned to start at the top floor and work his way down, sort of take his time, explore the place, see what there was to see. But he'd not been prepared for the empty floor when he'd seen it from the elevator. Now, as he prowled the darkened hallway, he laughed silently at his luck.

Piles of mattresses, desks, and cartons blocked the central passageway. He picked his way carefully past their shadowy hulks, peering into rooms and closets, his senses alert for any sound beyond the squish of his sneakers on the linoleum.

He heard the sound of dripping water and followed it into an alcove, counting the rhythm as fat droplets splashed into a rusting sink. Denny knew it would be easy to find a wrench and fix the offending drip. It would be easy, in fact, to find whatever he needed to suit his simple needs.

He groped his way along an inner corridor, looking for the central stairway. He would have to settle himself where he could get out quickly if anyone entered the floor. He peered around; the more he thought about it, the surer he was that he could live up here undetected.

Thinking of the stairs, he remembered the elevator and made his way back to it, anxious to move it before anyone noticed it had stopped on the twelfth floor. Besides, he'd been gone from his bed long enough. It was time to get back down. That Danziger, the morning nurse, had given him the creeps once, staring at him the way she had when she thought he was asleep. He couldn't afford to call attention to himself the way he had in Santa Barbara, especially now, when divine providence had led him to this empty floor.

He rode the elevator down to seven, just to be on the safe side, then took the stairs one flight down and peered out into the hallway. There were plenty of people around; visiting hours were in full swing. It would be easy to blend in with the crowd of visitors and make his way to his room, slip into the washroom, and change quickly from his clothes to the hospital gown.

By the time Danziger poked her head into the room Denny was back in bed, covered to his chin, staring at the ceiling, planning his next move.

Glenn Walters stared sullenly at the last of the Rorschach ink blots. 'It's a little girl,' he said at last. 'A little girl with pigtails. Somebody hacked off both her legs. She's bleeding all over the place.'

Margie wordlessly stacked the cards. He was still trying to shock her. She felt sure he had not given an honest response since she'd begun the series of tests.

'I think that's enough for now,' she said. 'Would you like to talk for a while?'

Glenn folded his arms and leaned back

in his chair. 'No. There's nothing to talk about. I took your dumb tests; now leave me alone. I won't be here much longer, anyway.'

'I see,' Margie said. 'Where will you be?'

'It's none of your damn business. I talked to my new lawyer last night. He's getting me out of here. He said he'd make sure I was nice and comfy until we go back to court.'

Margie had heard nothing more from Carlton Richards to indicate he was planning to move his client. Until she did, she was going to proceed as she would with any other patient.

'Tell me, Glenn, as long as you're leaving, what would you like to do when this is over? Get a job, go back to school, go back to Arizona, what?'

'All I want is to be left alone. Go where I want when I want. When people try to order me around, it makes me want to punch them out.'

Margie believed she'd finally heard a truthful response from Glenn Walters. 'Is that why you killed Anna Hardesty's cat? Did she try to order you around?'

Hate flared in Glenn's expression and just as quickly faded. 'No way, lady. You're not gonna bait me. I told you, I'm out of this place?'

'And then what?'

'Then I tell the judge how sorry I am and I'm gone, free as a bird.'

'Are you sorry?'

'What do you think?'

'I don't know. That's why I asked you.'

Glenn's face was a mockery of a little-boy pout. 'I—am—sorry—as—hell.'

Margie pressed. 'Sorry for what? Sorry that you killed the cat?'

'What else?' Glenn shrugged.

'What if the woman dies?'

Glenn's eyes narrowed. 'Old ladies die. You get old and you die.'

Margie was struck by how similar the words were to the words Carlton Richards had used. But Anna Hardesty wasn't dead yet. She might have a story to tell. More than ever, Margie wanted to know about Glenn's past in Arizona.

'Glenn, do you have a high school diploma?'

'I passed an equivalency test.'

'In Scottsdale?'

'Yeah. It's none of your business, but now you know I'm not stupid.'

Margie smiled. 'I know you're not stupid. You took an IQ test yesterday, remember?'

'Oh, yeah. How'd I do?'

'I'll tell you how you did, if you'll tell me something, first. If you're so anxious to be out on your own, how come you chose to stay on with your parents after you turned eighteen?'

Glenn shrugged, but his face was animated. 'First of all, they're not my *parents*. I never had a father. I only had a mother. And she crapped out after she married Walters.'

'I see,' Margie said. 'You were only six. Can you remember that far back?'

'Sure,' Glenn said. 'I remember everything.'

'What do you remember most?'

Glenn fidgeted. 'I don't know. Lots of things. She used to sing me to sleep. An Irish song, at least she said it was Irish. She sang to me every night.'

Margie watched his expression soften. 'Then what happened?' she asked.

'Then she got married. He was a drunk. He hit her. And he wouldn't let her sing. She wouldn't sing to me. Not even if I begged... I used to think if she would sing me to sleep, everything would be okay.'

'But it wasn't okay.'

Glenn's eyes grew flinty. 'What's the difference? It doesn't matter. When I get my money, I'm going to split. It doesn't matter anymore.'

'What money is that, Glenn?'

'Money that's mine. Walters can't lay a hand on it.'

Margie let that pass. 'You don't like your stepfather.'

'What was your first clue?'

She decided to gamble. 'Did he stand by you when you got into trouble in Scottsdale?'

Glenn's face darkened, his jaw clenched, but he fought to maintain control. 'You asked me questions. I gave you answers. Tell me how I did on the test.'

Margie nodded, noting once again how volatile Glenn Walters was and how quickly he'd moved from stony silence to melancholy to anger. But she'd learned a lot. 'All right,' she said. 'One twenty on the Stanford-Binet.'

'That's good?'

'That's good.'

The slow, curved smile. 'I knew it. I'm smarter than anyone.'

Dr Joseph Landesmann had five minutes before he was due in surgery.

Heaving his bulk into the ancient desk chair, he removed his glasses and spent one full minute kneading his throbbing temples. Then he put his glasses back on and reached for the list he had requested from Medical Records.

Discharge orders for nine of the seventy-two patients who'd left Vejar State Hospital on September 23 were signed by him. The

106

names of these nine were underlined in red as he had specified, but Landesmann scanned them one by one and frowned. Not one of them seemed even vaguely familiar.

'Damn,' he muttered, pursing fleshy lips. 'Damn anonymous medicine. They come, they go, the ulcer, the gall bladder. How the hell do I know who they are?'

Angry with himself, he glanced at his watch and read through the list again: Baker, Dalgliesh, Gonzales, Kiefer, Mendez, Noonan, Thienh, Velasquez, Wein.

Mendez and Wein, he could eliminate them. He remembered they'd had large families, who'd managed to track him down at all hours for updates on the patients' condition. There was no reason for him to have written the name of a shelter on cards he'd given to them.

Dalgliesh, too, an appendectomy, and Gonzales; the two were roommates. Their wives had gone together and brought in a box of candy on the morning the patients were discharged. And Thienh was a woman, a Vietnamese who'd invited him to eat at her restaurant.

That left only four. Landesmann studied the list, beginning to enjoy the puzzle. He could request records on all four, of course, jog his memory with them. But he was close. Concentrate...Kiefer...Kiefer...A face swam into his consciousness.

A youngish man. Some sort of bellyache of ideopathic origin. He remembered the face, sweating, nervous. He'd sat right here in this office.

Landesmann smiled, proud of himself. He did remember the guy. The one who'd almost decked a nurse, nearly ended up in the psych ward. Oregon. The kid was going to a lumber camp and needed a place to stay. Yes! He had used the back of a card to write down the name of a shelter.

The doctor had his hand on the phone when it shrilled, a raucous blare. 'Landesmann. Yes, I'll be right there. All right, I'm on my way.'

He broke the connection, picked up again, and began to unbutton his coat. 'Medical Records, can you make it snappy?' He loosened his tie.

'Medical Records.'

'Dr Landesmann on four. I need you to send up a file. Kiefer, K-i-e-f-e-r, first name Dennis. Got it?'

'Yes, sir. Dr Landesmann?'

'Just send it up. I'm on my way to surgery.'

'Yes, sir. But, sir? Do you want the whole file? Or just the last admittance?'

Landesmann heard a knock at his door. In seconds, a scrub nurse peered in.

'Dr Landesmann? They're waiting.'

'Yes, yes, I know.' He could feel his blood pressure rising. 'Send the whole damn file!' he said into the phone.

'Yes, sir, I will. Dr Landesmann?'

'What?'

'My computer shows Mr Kiefer never signed out when you discharged him on September twenty-third. We could have a problem with state reimbursement if—'

'Just send up the file!' he roared.

The scrub nurse backed out.

The clerk hung up.

His temples were pounding again.

CHAPTER 10

It was ten minutes of four and Margie was anxious to get home to Trisha and the baby, but there was time to make a couple of quick phone calls before she called it a day.

She called Good Samaritan Hospital first, but there was no change in the condition of Anna Hardesty, the owner of the cat Glenn had tortured. The woman remained in a semicoma, still hooked to a respirator to help her breathe, unable to respond to questions.

Next she dialled Information in Scottsdale, Arizona, and requested two telephone numbers. It was too late to reach anyone at the high school, so she dialled the second number.

'County offices,' a woman said.

Margie asked for juvenile records. She held through three selections of elevator music before someone came on the line.

'Hello,' she said finally. 'This is Margie Reed. I'm a forensic psychologist at Santa Clarita State Hospital in California, and I have requested juvenile records on a man named Glenn Walters. I wondered if you'd received my request and how quickly I may expect information.'

The man's voice was whiny and nasal. 'Requests for records from out of state are processed in the order in which they are received. If you sent your request through proper channels, it should take four to six weeks.'

Margie grimaced. 'This will have to be expedited. I don't have four to six weeks to wait. Walters has been arraigned on felony charges in California and I need to complete a report for the court.'

The man she spoke to was not impressed. 'I know of no way to expedite it. If you sent your request through proper channels, it should take four to six weeks.'

I might as well be talking to a recording, Margie thought. 'Thanks a million,' she

110

said and hung up.

She drummed her fingernails on the surface of her desk. There was more than one way to skin a cat. 'Oh!' she put a hand over her face. 'Of all the damned expressions to use!'

'Are you sleeping or thinking?'

Margie looked up to see Chet Anderson in her doorway, holding a cup of coffee in each hand. 'Neither,' she said. 'I was chewing myself out for using a thoroughly tasteless idiom.'

'Oh,' Chet said, handing her a cup and pushing up his glasses. 'May that be the biggest mistake you ever make. Here, I wish I'd thought to bring some cheese Danish from Harry's Deli, but maybe you can use this.'

'Thanks,' Margie said, flipping off the lid. 'Come to think of it, I don't think I had lunch.'

'Neither did I. I lost my appetite when I smelled the sweat socks burning.'

Margie looked up.

'It's Friday, isn't it? Must have been tuna supreme. Whatever it was, the smell wafted up and killed off my lust for lunch.'

'It *is* Friday.' Margie sipped her coffee and glanced over at her notepad.

'You make it sound bad.'

'No, no, not really. These calls will

have to wait, that's all.' She glanced at her watch. 'And if that's the case, I might as well get home to my guests.'

'Actually,' Chet said. 'That's why I stopped in. I thought we could all go to dinner, including the baby. I'd love to escort the three prettiest women in the state.'

Margie looked at his earnest face. She knew she was going to hurt his feelings, but she needed to have some time alone with Trisha so that they could talk.

'Chet,' she said carefully. 'I appreciate the offer. But I need some time alone with Trisha. She didn't travel three thousand miles just to make the visit. She's got trouble at home, and maybe I can help. Tell me you understand.'

'Sure,' he said. 'Another time. Just sounded like a good idea.' He smiled, capping his empty cup, but he looked like a wounded pup.

It occurred to Margie to cheer him up by inviting him to dinner on Sunday. The words teetered on the tip of her tongue, but they wouldn't tumble out.

What's the matter with me? She managed a smile, but her face felt almost wooden. 'Thanks,' she murmured. 'Another time. Maybe early next week.'

Chet tossed back his lank blond hair and gave a chipper salute from the doorway.

'Well,' he said, 'have a good weekend. I hope it all works out for Trisha.'

'You, too,' she said, but he was already gone. She stared at the empty doorway. She had the odd feeling she'd crossed a threshold, but she didn't know what it was.

The weather had cooled a little in the aftermath of the Santa Ana winds, and already the smog pushed thickly against the mountains, nearly obscuring them from view.

Margie turned the air conditioning on low and backed out of her parking space, deciding she would stop at a local convenience store to pick up fixings for dinner.

She bought thick-sliced ham and German potato salad, a couple of red, ripe tomatoes, and half a honeydew melon, stacking them all in a rickety cart and heading towards the register. Then she remembered that Trisha was nursing Rebecca, and she picked up two cartons of low-fat milk and a package of Oreo cookies, in case Trisha was one of those people who thought milk was invented to go with cookies.

Tomorrow she would do some serious marketing, stocking up on fruits and vegetables as well as things for Sunday's dinner. She had no idea how long Trisha was apt to stay, but while she was here, Margie determined, she was going to eat right.

Maybe, she thought, paying for her purchases and loading the groceries into her car, Trisha had called Rob and worked it out so that things were better between them. Margie had left her office number at home, but her sister-in-law had not called her, and Margie had resisted the urge to phone home for fear of waking the baby.

She slipped her key into the apartment door's lock, careful to avert her gaze from the police notice posted on the corner apartment. Balancing the grocery bags, she set her purse down and closed the door with her foot.

'Trish?' she called softly, putting down her bundles to lock the door. 'Hi, Trisha, I'm home.'

'We're in the kitchen,' Trisha called back. It was then Margie caught a whiff of something good and realized how hungry she was.

'Hi!' she said, setting the groceries down on the small kitchen table. 'God, it smells good in here! Rebecca, hey, sweetie babe, what have you and Mommy been doing?'

Rebecca was propped on a pillow on the floor, happily flailing a plastic measuring spoon. She smiled delightedly as Margie scooped her up and cuddled her close against her.

'We figured you'd be hungry, so we rummaged around and put a little something together,' Trish said, removing a casserole from the oven. 'Your timing's perfect. Gourmet it isn't. You keep a pretty skinny larder.'

'I know,' Margie said. 'Sorry about that. I mostly live on salads and yogurt. Occasionally I get these crazy cravings and pig out on slippy, gloppy burgers, but in between I figure I'll behave a little better if I don't keep temptation in the cupboard.'

Trisha poured salad dressing on a bowl of greens and began to toss it lightly. 'Well, I found some tuna and soup and stuff, so I put together a casserole. My mother called it emergency rations, but it always does in a pinch.'

Margie smiled, remembering what Chet had said about the tuna supreme in the cafeteria. She guessed she had been too busy to notice it earlier, but the sweat socks smell had lingered in the air as Margie waited for the elevator, and whatever Trisha had cobbled up was not even in the same ball park.

'It smells wonderful,' she said, turning her head away as Rebecca grabbed for her earring. 'Hey, baby-cakes, are you lucky to have a mama who can cook!'

She took the baby's tiny hand and marvelled at its silky softness. Rebecca looked at her with great round eyes and gave her a toothless grin.

'I'll feed Rebecca while you put the groceries away,' Trisha said. 'We won't be long. I'll take her in the bedroom, so I can change her diaper, too.'

Margie surrendered the sweet-smelling baby and watched with admiration as Trisha slung her expertly on one hip and headed down the hall.

'Oh,' her sister-in-law said, turning around. 'I almost forgot to tell you. You either got flowers from Dracula's garden or somebody really goofed.'

'What happened?' Margie asked.

Trisha made a face. 'I was feeding the baby, sometime around noon, and I heard the doorbell ring. When I got to the door I asked who it was, twice, but nobody answered. So I left the chain on, unlocked the door and took a peek outside—and I saw what looked like some kind of flower arrangement leaning against the wall.'

'A flower arrangement.'

'Yes,' Trisha said. 'So I opened up the door. It was flowers, all right.' Her eyes widened. 'Funeral flowers, you know? Like calla lilies and all that stuff, made into a wreath and all draped up in black?'

Margie frowned. 'Must have been a

mistake. Maybe they were misdelivered.'

'That's what I thought,' Trisha agreed. 'So I checked to see if there was a card. There was, but all it said was, "Rest in peace." There was no name, no sender, no nothing.'

'That is a little strange,' Margie agreed. 'Did you call the florist who sent them?'

'I would have if I could have,' Trisha said. 'There was nothing with the florist's name, either.'

Rebecca, who had been chewing on her little fist, began to fidget in Trisha's arms. Trisha began a rocking motion. 'The whole thing seemed a little weird.'

'Hmm,' said Margie. 'So, where are the flowers?'

Rebecca began to cry.

Trisha shrugged. 'I finally figured they might have been meant for'—she paused— 'the girl who died next door, although why they'd come here instead of to the funeral home is sure beyond me. Anyway, I ended up calling your superintendent, and I gave the flowers to him. Who knows, somebody might inquire whether the flowers were ever delivered.'

Margie nodded. 'Good idea. Undoubtedly, someone will. Go take care of Screaming Mimi. I'll get dinner on the table.'

Trisha retreated down the hall. Margie unpacked the groceries. She set the table with her best linens and poured two glasses of milk. Finished, she wondered if Trisha would mind if she watched her feed the baby.

She was halfway down the hall when she heard Trisha singing and she stopped in her tracks to listen. It was 'Summertime,' from Gershwin's *Porgy and Bess*. Trisha's high sweet soprano and the love that she poured into every note brought tears to Margie's eyes.

'She wouldn't sing to me,' Glenn Walters had said. 'Not even if I begged. I used to think if she would sing me to sleep, everything would be okay...'

When the song ended, Margie swallowed hard and tapped at the open door. 'Mind if I come in? Please don't stop singing. It's lovely, really lovely.'

'Of course, come in,' Trisha said softly. 'She's just about out, anyway. It doesn't matter if I sing to her or not. Full tummy and she's out like a light.'

Rebecca lay in her mother's arms, her head lolling to one side, a fan of lashes under closed eyes, her rosebud mouth in a pout.

'Sometimes I fall asleep along with her,' Trisha said.

'I know. You did last night.'

Her sister-in-law shrugged. 'Well, why not? Rob's usually not around anyway.'

118

Trisha laid the baby in the centre of the bed and arranged the pillows around her. 'Come,' she said. 'Let's have dinner. We can talk while we eat.'

Margie helped herself to salad and passed the bowl to Trisha. 'Did you call Rob?' she asked. 'I mean, it's none of my business, but just to let him know where you are.'

'Yes,' Trisha said, serving the casserole. 'And I'm glad I did. He was worried, but that's okay. Let him stew. I've worried enough about him.'

'Look.' Margie put down her fork. 'I want you to know two things. The first is that you're welcome to stay here just as long as you like. The second is that I won't interfere—that is, unless you want me to. I'm Rob's sister and I'm your friend, but I also happen to be a psychologist. You tell me if I start to get clinical, and I promise I'll shut up.'

Trisha smiled, filling her plate. 'You don't think I came here 'cause I like you? Heck, not everybody's favourite sister-in-law happens to be a shrink! It's okay, Margie. I'll talk. You listen. Then tell me what you think.'

Margie took a bite of tuna casserole. 'Yummy. Okay, talk.'

'I want you to know this is hard for me, Margie, mostly because I know it's going to dredge up painful memories for you, too,' Trisha said. 'But whether we want to think about it or not, the trouble started after Frank died.'

'I see.' Margie poked at her salad. 'Tell me what you mean by trouble.'

Trisha sighed. 'I don't know exactly how to say this, Margie, but Rob must have been keeping up a brave front as long as you were around.'

'He was wonderful for me,' Margie said softly. 'You were, too. I never told you, but I don't know how I would have made it through those first weeks if it hadn't been for the two of you.'

'I know,' Trisha said. 'If the situation had been reversed, you would have been there for us, too. The fact is, after you left for California, Rob just seemed to fall apart. It's like he was able to hang in there as long as he thought you needed him. But once you were gone, he—I don't know. He couldn't seem to handle anything. He started drinking—'

'Drinking? Rob?'

Trisha nodded. 'A lot. But that didn't last too long. Then he started coming home real late, like he didn't want to be around me.'

Margie shook her head. 'That's hard to believe. He was so happy about the baby coming.'

'He hasn't been happy about anything,

Margie. Even when Rebecca was born. He came to see us once in the hospital and he didn't come back until it was time to take us home. He said he was extra busy at work. But that's another thing—money's been real tight, so I don't think that was true. Anyway, he wouldn't be out showing property at two or three o'clock in the morning.'

Margie pushed food around on her plate. It was hard to believe they were talking about her brother. Not Rob, who'd wanted to marry Trisha so much that he'd dropped out of college in his second year, got his realtor's licence, and within six months managed to build a handsome clientele.

But Trisha was far too practical to exaggerate, and it had been nearly dawn when Rob had phoned her.

'Did you talk?' Margie asked.

'When he would talk,' Trisha grimaced. 'But that wasn't very often. Every now and then, he'd promise to change his ways. He would, for a little while. Then he'd clam up again and start staying out late. Even when I threatened to leave.'

Margie considered. Another woman? Trisha would have said that if she thought it. She looked directly at her sister-in-law. 'What do you think is the problem?'

'Guilt.' Trisha's answer was quick and

succinct. 'I think he feels guilty about Frank.'

Margie nodded. She'd dealt with survivors who felt guilty after the death of a loved one—even in cases where there was nothing they could have done to prevent the death from occurring.

'I know what you're thinking,' Trisha said. 'I begged him to see a psychologist. I wanted to call you, ask you to recommend someone, but Rob absolutely refused. He didn't want you to know anything about it. He said you'd been hurt enough—'

Trisha's doll-like blue eyes filled with tears. She brushed away the fat droplets with a small, freckled hand. 'He's right, you know. I shouldn't be bothering you. I just didn't know what else to do...'

Margie felt her own tears coming and moved toward Trisha, but the telephone rang, loud in the silence, constant, obstinate, demanding.

'Hello,' she said, fully expecting to give whoever it was short shrift. Then, as she listened, she closed her eyes and struggled to regain her control.

'It's the hospital,' she told Trisha, weighing what she had just heard against reluctance to leave her sister-in-law alone. 'One of my patients got into it with an inmate. They want me to come back if I can.'

'Go,' said Trisha. 'We'll be fine. I'll bolt the door. Don't worry.'

Margie wavered.

'Please,' Trisha said. 'Margie, it's your job.'

Margie sighed. 'I won't be long. Don't open the door for *anyone.*'

CHAPTER 11

It was seven thirty in the evening when Dr Landesmann left the surgical wing, and closer to eight by the time he'd showered and changed—later by an hour or more than he was accustomed to being at Vejar on a Friday.

The gall bladder that should have been routine turned out be an anaesthetic nightmare, and then there was the emergency, the kid who flipped his cycle. The boy would need a miracle to last the night despite three hours on the table.

Landesmann shook his head as he unlocked his office. Damn fool kids, they wouldn't wear helmets!

He expected to be in the office just long enough to call his wife and pick up his medical bag, but when he turned on the desk lamp he saw the Kiefer file lying there, and he eased himself into his chair.

Kiefer, as the doctor thought he remembered, was indeed the bellyache, a transient admitted from the ER complaining of intestinal pain. He was treated and released two days later, although an indignant entry in red ink appended by the cashier's office indicated the patient had not signed discharge forms absolving the hospital from further liability.

What Landesmann had not recalled earlier, which flooded back to him now, was that Kiefer was the patient who'd had to be restrained from physically attacking a nurse. That was why he'd considered moving him to the psych ward for observation.

He envisioned Kiefer, a tall, thin, sandy-haired man in his mid-twenties with a scraggly beard that did little to conceal the scars of teenage acne—the kid who told him he had a job waiting at some lumber camp up in Oregon.

Landesmann leaned back in his chair, crossing his hands over his abdomen, and gazed out through his office window into the dark and starless night.

The hospital corridors had buzzed with apprehension and outrage on the day the gardener's body was discovered in a flower bed on the seaward side of the building.

The doctor deliberated whether Kiefer might be capable of that kind of brutal violence, and, remembering the incident with the nurse, he wondered whether he'd erred in electing not to detain him.

He did not specifically recall giving Kiefer one of his cards, or writing the address of the Salvation Army Shelter on the back of it—although he had certainly done that kind of thing in the past for transients he was about to discharge. But according to the detective, Landesmann's card had turned up in proximity with the dead gardener's jewellery. Given the short fuse Kiefer had displayed on the ward, lunging at a nurse for being slow to respond to a call signal, Landesmann conceded that the man might indeed be violent.

Curious, he rummaged through the file that had been sent up by Medical Records. He saw that Kiefer had been admitted to Vejar on two prior occasions: once for a three-day period early in June and once for two days five months earlier. On both occasions the patient had been admitted from the ER for similar complaints: intestinal tract disorders of unknown origin causing cramps, vomiting, and diarrhoea.

Landesmann drummed his fingers on the desk top. That struck him as odd. Transients, by nature, rarely stayed long in one area, and for Kiefer to have been admitted three times in eight months was unusual, to say the least.

Vejar, being a state hospital, was one of few facilities in the Santa Barbara area that accepted vagrants at all, treating them under Medi-Cal guidelines and billing the state for reimbursement. But if Keifer was a transient with a lengthy history of intestinal problems, he might have also sought treatment elsewhere in the state. It occurred to Landesmann that state reimbursement records might be of use to the police.

He glanced at his watch and knew it was too late to do anything about that tonight. On Monday he would call and request Kiefer's records from the office in Sacramento. Now, he thought he might try to reach the officer who'd called him from Santa Barbara P.D. Rummaging on his desk for the note he'd scribbled to himself, he picked up the phone and dialled.

'Desk, Adams,' a voice answered.

He asked for Detective Nance.

'Detective Nance is off duty till Monday. Would you like to speak to someone else?'

Landesmann debated. It was late already. His wife was going to be livid.

'No,' he said. 'Leave a message. Dr Landesmann at Vejar State Hospital.'

126

Sixty miles down the coast, at Santa Clarita State Hospital, Margie took an elevator to the eleventh floor and pressed a buzzer to request admittance to the forensics ward.

'I'm Margie Reed,' she told the night guard, showing her identification through the square of glass in the door. 'I was called about a problem with Glenn Walters.'

'Yes, ma'am.' A beefy guard let her in. 'He's quiet now, but that boy's got a temper! Took two officers to hold him back and get him into his cell.'

'The altercation took place in the corridor?'

'Yes, ma'am. The inmates were on their way to shower. All of a sudden, Walters bolts the line and takes a punch at O'Toole—you know the one I mean? The big guy who has the cell across from Walters.'

Margie nodded. She knew O'Toole. He was Chet's patient and twice the size of Glenn. 'I'll see Walters in his cell,' she said. 'Tell the officer I'm on my way.'

The guard picked up a phone, and by the time she crossed the hall, the heavy door had swung open.

The officer who greeted her was young and black, with the muscular forearms of a wrestler. He shook her hand. 'Maynard

Pace,' he said. 'I'm the officer who called you. Actually, now I don't guess I needed to. Walters has quieted down. Sorry if I brought you on a wild goose chase. For a while, he was a real wildcat.'

'It's okay,' Margie said. 'As long as I'm here, I'll go ahead and see him. I know the fight broke out in the shower line. Do you have any idea what started it?'

The officer flashed her a chagrined smile. 'Haven't got to the bottom of it yet. One minute the guys were marching along, the next minute Walters was swinging. O'Toole swears up and down he didn't provoke it, but you know how that goes. I'll talk to him some more. You can too, if you want. I'll have a report for you by Monday.'

Margie nodded. 'That'll be fine.' She moved down the dimly lighted hall. Pace unlocked Glenn's cell and Margie went inside, her eyes adjusting to the shadows.

Glenn was stretched out on his side on the cot, his face against the wall. She drew up a stool and sat beside the bed. 'Glenn,' she said. 'Are you awake?'

There was no answer, but Margie guessed by his ragged breathing that her patient was very much awake.

'It's Margie Reed,' she said. 'I heard there was a problem. A fight. Do you want to talk about it?'

Again, no answer. Margie persisted.

128

'Why did you want to hit O'Toole?'

She waited, but Glenn did not move a muscle.

'Look,' she said firmly. 'I came back to the ward because I thought you might want to talk to me. If you don't want to talk, then I'm wasting my time, so I'll tell you what I'm going to do. I will count silently from zero to fifty. You have that long to make up your mind. If you don't turn around by the time I count fifty, I will leave, and I mean what I say.'

She began to count and it seemed to her that Glenn's tension was palpable. Nineteen ... twenty ... twenty-one ... His breathing had begun to slow.

Thirty-six ... thirty-seven ... thirty-eight ... thirty-nine... She heard him shift on the cot.

On the count of fifty, Margie rose and moved the stool back against the wall. Her own footsteps seemed loud in the silence. She wondered if the other inmates were asleep.

She was one step from the door of the cell when she heard a muffled sound behind her.

'I asked him to stop. But he wouldn't. He wouldn't. He just kept singing that song...the Irish one my mother used to sing. I just had to shut...him...up...'

Five floors below them, in his hospital bed, Denny Kiefer stirred restlessly.

He had palmed the sleeping pill he'd been given earlier and now, lying awake in the eerie near-darkness, he listened to the wheezing night sounds of his roommates, and he forced himself to keep from slipping out of bed and going through their belongings.

It would be easy, so easy, to snag a watch or a ring, something he could hock for a little cash, then claim that a piece of his own jewellery was missing and finger an aide or an orderly.

It would work, he knew. He had done it before, hidden all sorts of things. But if he did it now, he would call attention to himself, and that was the last thing he wanted. He was anxious, agitated, ready to make a move, but the timing, he knew, would have to be perfect and he wanted to do it right.

He tossed uncomfortably in the soft bed. He almost wished he'd taken the sleeping pill, but he needed to be alert when the morning shift came on. He would want them to know he was being discharged, especially the jumpy broad, that nurse, Danziger. She was really getting on his nerves.

Denny turned again, punched a hollow in the pillow, and tried to settle in. But

130

he was too revved up, too eager to get on with it. Sleep was out of the question.

Finally, he knew what would calm him down. He slipped quietly out of bed and rummaged in the closet for the little cloth bag he kept in his jeans pocket.

In the small bathroom the tile floor was cold and there was barely enough space to hunker down, but Denny opened the little bag and began to spill out his treasures. He felt better right away when he picked up the first piece, the newest piece, the little opal ring the airline stewardess had worn.

He turned it round and round in his hand, rubbing the circle of gold, pleased with the way the stone flashed colour as he turned it this way and that.

One by one, he examined his prizes, his private little stock of souvenirs; the stick pin from the geezer on the river in Oregon who never knew what hit him, the class ring from the guy at the gas station who wouldn't open the till, and the pearl earrings from the woman in Sacramento. He'd warned her not to scream, but she wouldn't listen.

There was the delicate gold chain from the hiker in Modesto, that coiled into a glittering little heap, and the diamond stud he'd yanked from the ear of that badass dude on the beach. Denny smiled. They ought to give him a medal for offing *that* son of a bitch.

The only thing missing was the little silver cross he'd taken from the neck of the gardener. It made Denny angry that he hadn't remembered to take it from his jacket pocket—angrier still that he'd left the jacket, and the book bag, in the old man's car.

But that was okay. He could see it in his mind and imagine it was in his collection. It was going to be fun to make a place for his things when he moved to the deserted twelfth floor.

Reluctantly, Denny picked up each piece and dropped it into the bag, stuffed it deep in his jeans pocket, and groped his way back to bed.

He managed to doze a little, snapping awake when anyone entered the room. He was wide-eyed when the first blush of dawn bled into the inky night.

CHAPTER 12

It was barely light out when Margie rose groggily from the bed she'd made on the sofa, wondering how anybody as tiny as Rebecca could emit such piercing screams.

132

She could hear Trisha's reassuring murmurs, telling the baby she would wake her aunt Margie, and then there was an almost joyous silence as the baby found her breakfast. Margie smiled, leaning back on the sofa. Trisha had a talent for motherhood.

At first she thought she might go back to sleep, but when she found she couldn't, Margie reached for her robe, padded to the kitchen, and put on a pot of coffee. Then she found her slippers, unlocked the door, and went out to get the morning paper.

It was chilly outside. Margie hoped that fall was on its way—at least the version of it that people told her passed for fall in Southern California. She could manage to live without snow, she thought, if at least there was a chill in the air.

Her gaze fell on the police notice sealing the apartment next door, and she paused, wondering how long it would be before the grim reminder was removed. Unable to stop herself, she turned her head and looked up into the stairwell. It was empty, but she felt uneasy and she stared for a long time.

Then she bent down to pick up the newspaper, but she dropped it and drew back, gasping, her eyes focusing on the still body of a tiny brown bird.

Its eyes were open, but its little head was

twisted at an odd angle, and something that looked like dried blood caked its tiny beak. Margie shuddered. Probably some cat had caught the poor thing and toyed with it till it got bored. But here it was, and now she was going to have to figure out what to do with it.

'Margie?'

She heard Trisha calling and she looked around quickly. There was nothing for it but to wrap the bird in newspaper and throw it into the trash.

'I'll be right there, Trisha,' Margie called. 'I just came out to find the paper.'

Quickly she pulled some classified pages out of the bulky *Times,* enveloped the tiny corpse, and carried it to the barrels downstairs. Then, shivering inside her robe, she went back to her own apartment.

'Margie, I'm sorry. We woke you, didn't we?' Trisha patted Rebecca's bottom. 'You munchkin, I told you you'd wake your aunt Margie. And here it is barely six o'clock!'

Margie hurried past them into the kitchen and quickly scrubbed her hands, trying hard to wash away the image of the poor mangled bird. Then she reached for the smiling baby. 'It's okay, I forgive you this time.'

She buried her face in Rebecca's little

chest and breathed in the scent of talcum powder.

'I smell coffee!' Trisha sniffed, making a beeline for the kitchen. 'You play with the baby. I'll get us coffee. It's the least I can do by way of penance.'

She brought in two cups and set one down on the table in front of Margie. 'I feel kind of bad putting you out of bed. Are you sure you don't want us to sleep out here?'

Margie shook her head. 'Not a chance. You and the baby need the bedroom. Besides, it's pretty comfy out here. That's not a bad sofa at all.'

'It's a lovely sofa,' Trisha said, beginning to fold the sheets. 'It's a nice apartment. You've done a great job. It really feels like home.'

Margie patted the drowsing Rebecca and looked around her living room. She had chosen her furnishings very quickly and without a lot of enthusiasm, but now she was pleased, surprised, really, to see how well they worked—a casual blend of mauve and grey and a great profusion of plants.

'Thanks,' she said. 'To tell you the truth, I never gave it much thought. But it is comfortable and I'm glad you like it. I guess it feels like home.'

Trisha sat, the bed linens stacked in a haphazard pile on her lap. 'Margie,' she said, 'are you okay?' Her wide, blue eyes were earnest. 'I mean, here I come, with all my problems, and I don't even know how you're doing. It's just that you're the closest family we have. I didn't know where else to go.'

'I'm fine,' Margie said, brushing a finger against Rebecca's silky cheek. 'Mostly, I try not to think about the past. Or if I do, to remember the good times. It isn't easy making a new life, but I think I'm making progress. I'm glad you came here. I've missed you and Rob, and I'm tickled pink to see Rebecca!'

Trisha nodded. 'Rob called last night while you were back at the hospital. He said he misses us very much and he asked me when we were coming home.'

'What did you tell him?'

'That I miss him, too, but I'm not ready to go home. He has to get help. He has to get himself together. Things can't be the way they were.'

Margie smiled. 'That took a lot of strength, but I think you did the right thing. Now he'll have to think it through and decide to make the next move.'

Gently she eased the dozing baby onto a blanket on the floor. Then she straightened and put an arm around Trisha. 'So tell me, how are you?'

'I'm fine.' Trisha gave her a shaky grin.

'I'll be better if I have some breakfast.'

'Right. Then we'll take the baby out for some air and go to the grocery store. I forgot to tell you, I invited someone to join us for Sunday dinner.'

Trisha looked at her. 'Who?' she asked.

'Paul Sellers. The lieutenant you met.'

'Really.' Trisha's smile grew impish. 'Well, what do you know about that?'

Paul Sellers woke up Saturday morning determined not to think about work, but he had not been up for more than ten minutes when he got a call from the lab.

'Missed you at the station last night,' Ken Kramer told him. 'I thought you'd want to know that we picked up prints all over Kerns's living room that could belong to your man—and some hair samples and fibres we'll keep on tap till you're ready to go for a match.'

It was not the first time the lab technician had pried him out of bed on a weekend, but for reasons he couldn't have put into words, Paul found himself vaguely annoyed. 'Okay,' he said. 'Send the prints over. We'll run 'em through the system on Monday.'

He could almost see the technician's face. 'Monday?' Kramer said.

'Yeah. Ever hear of a weekend off? I decided I'm overdue.'

137

Kramer paused. 'So okay. Enjoy. Sorry if I woke you up.'

Paul grimaced. 'You didn't wake me. And thanks. It's the first good news I've had.'

'You're welcome, I'm sure.' Kramer was miffed. 'That's why the county pays me.'

Paul would have suggested that they get together for a tall one later in the week, but Kramer hung up and Paul felt worse, hearing the broken connection. Finally he slammed down his own receiver and stormed into the kitchen, opening and slamming shut cabinet doors looking for his favourite skillet.

When he finally found it, he set to work making the perfect omelette. Three eggs and cheese. Cholesterol be damned. He was going to enjoy this weekend. But after he ate, he felt like a jerk. What in the hell was bugging him?

He had cleaned up the kitchen, made the bed, and begun to run the vacuum when the answer came to him, face to face from a silver frame on the mantel. Jamie and Donna were smiling broadly from the last portrait they'd had taken.

Jamie was frozen there, forever four, a mischievous, bright-eyed kid. Paul could almost feel him squirming under his mother's hand.

He stood there, looking at the four-year-old portrait. 'It's not a date,' he said. 'I'm only going for Sunday dinner. Her sister-in-law will be there, too.'

Donna smiled at him from her place on the mantel. *Four years,* he could hear her say. *Enough already. But if you wear that green sport coat, I'll never speak to you again.*

Paul laughed out loud. How she hated that sport coat. He began to push the vacuum. When he finished cleaning, he was going out and buy himself something new...blue, maybe, a navy blue blazer and maybe some light grey slacks....

Timing was everything and Denny knew that his was going to be perfect.

He was ready for action when the first of the cleaning crew came on at seven thirty, and he watched as they mopped the floors and collected the soiled linens.

They would move fast, trying to be finished before the doctors made their rounds. When the orderlies arrived to distribute the breakfast trays, Denny would have his chance.

Making the most of the morning bustle, he got up out of bed and sauntered casually into the hallway to observe the daily routine.

Nurses and aides moved in every

direction, darting in and out of rooms, deftly dodging the buckets and carts that littered the narrow hallway. Denny watched, feeling the rhythm, feeling his heartbeat quicken, picking his way amid the clutter until he found what he was looking for.

Stuffing a bundle under his gown, he glanced once around, then headed for the elevator, urging it up, willing it to arrive quickly.

It was empty. Denny got in gingerly and got off on the tenth floor, then took the stairs up two more flights, where he tossed his bundle to safety. In minutes he was back on the sixth floor, getting into bed, pouring cornflakes into a bowl, adding sugar and milk.

He was fully dressed when the doctor got there, a definite edge, he knew; he thanked him earnestly, said he felt great, and thanked him for everything again.

The balding doctor barely looked up, just made some notes on a chart, and mumbled something about discharge papers to be signed at the first-floor desk.

It was so easy, so smooth, that Denny felt euphoric, but he made a point of saying good-bye to every nurse on the floor.

'Thanks,' he said. 'Thanks for everything.' He even shook a few hands. 'You people are great. Nice to know you. Thanks. Thanks again.'

The nurses looked at him as though he'd lost his mind, but Denny didn't care. He wanted them all to know he was leaving, gone from the hospital for good. He was still smiling as he boarded the elevator and waved a jaunty good-bye.

On the first floor he found the right desk and waited patiently in line. When it was his turn, he smiled at the redheaded clerk. 'Kiefer. I've just been discharged.'

He waited whilst she checked a computer screen, put some papers together, and handed him a clipboard.

'Sign here and here.' She made an X with her pen in two places on the form. Denny signed. She turned the form over. 'And here.' She made another X.

Denny nodded and signed his name again. 'That's it?'

'That's it,' she said.

'Yeah. Well, thanks. And have a nice day.'

She looked up and over his shoulder. 'Right. Listen, if there's nothing else, you're holding up the line.'

Denny smiled, moved away from the desk, and strolled across the crowded lobby. He rode the elevator to the eleventh floor and took the stairs up to twelve.

He stood for a moment, letting his eyes adjust to the sudden dimness. Then he breathed in the musty air. 'Home, sweet home,' he said.

CHAPTER 13

Margie filled the last of the mushroom caps with stuffing, put the baking dish into the oven, and set the timer for twenty minutes.

She watched Trisha peeling vegetables at the sink. 'God, it smells good in here,' she said. 'I haven't done this much cooking since I moved to California. I'm surprised I remember how.'

Trisha looked up. 'Yankee pot roast is in your genes, like the colour of your eyes or your hair. You're right, it smells great. It's guaranteed to bowl the lieutenant over.'

Margie laughed. 'It was never intended to bowl anybody over.'

'Uh-huh. And neither was the lemon meringue pie you made from scratch this morning.'

Margie glanced at the fluffy pie, cooling on a rack on the counter. 'It's a simple thank-you, a little Sunday dinner to say "thanks for doing your job." '

Trisha rinsed the vegetables. 'Whatever you say. These are ready for the pot. I'm going in to change my clothes before the baby gets up.'

Margie scooped up the potatoes and carrots and added them to the roast. Why would she want to impress Paul Sellers? The idea struck her as absurd. She stirred the gravy, debating whether to wear her blue silk blouse or the yellow.

In the end she wore the pale yellow, softly shirred at the throat, with a pair of cocoa-coloured linen slacks and a pale yellow sash.

'Terr-rific,' Trisha said, watching Margie fluff her dark hair. 'Dynamite comes in a small package. Lieutenant Sellers, beware!'

'Stop it.' Margie swatted her playfully. 'Small packages, indeed. Look at you, with your tiny little waist, and here you are, a new mother.'

Trisha shrugged. 'Aerobics. I learned it from watching TV after Rebecca was born. With Rob gone so much, I had plenty of time until the baby started crying.'

As if on cue, Rebecca woke with a great, mournful wail.

'I'll get her,' Trisha said. 'You go check on your mushrooms. And stir the sour cream dip and put it in a dish to go with the raw veggies.'

'Yes, ma'am,' Margie said, laughing to

herself. Trisha reminded her of a mother hen with a helpless little chick in tow.

She had just finished arranging the hors d'oeuvres when she heard the telephone ring. *Damn,* she thought. *Not the hospital. I'm not going back there today.* She let it ring twice before picking it up. Then the doorbell rang.

'I'll get it.' Trisha went to the door, Rebecca slung on one hip.

'Hello,' Margie said into the phone. 'Oh, Rob, hello!' She covered one ear so she could hear her brother. 'Do you want to talk to Trisha?...I see. Yes, of course, I'll tell her... Okay, we'll see you then.'

Trisha bounded into the kitchen. 'Wine! Wasn't that sweet? Go say hello. He's in the living room. I can find the wineglasses.

Margie started to speak, changed her mind, and walked out into the living room, where Paul Sellers, balancing Rebecca, rose swiftly to his feet.

He was dressed smartly in a dark blue blazer, his trousers neatly creased. Margie saw that he handled the baby without a trace of awkwardness.

'Hi,' she said. 'This feels like a comedy. The phone and the doorbell at once.'

'Sorry.' His smile seemed to light his face. 'I seem to have rotten timing.'

Margie smiled back. 'It's not your fault. Here, let me take the baby. I'd really feel bad if she decided to burble all over your nice, clean jacket.'

She reached for Rebecca, but he took her hand. 'That's okay. I've got her. If she burbles, that's what babies do. Won't bother me at all.'

Margie felt the strength of his hand, saw the warmth in his eyes, and trembled a little, remembering sensations she thought she'd long forgotten.

'Well,' she said, sinking into a chair, 'then let's sit down, at least.' She watched him sit, propping Rebecca easily into the crook of his arm. She was glad when Trisha came into the room with three wineglasses on a tray.

If Paul was aware of his effect on her, he was gentleman enough not to show it. He accepted his wine and proposed a toast to happy Sunday afternoons.

'Here, here.' Trisha beamed, taking a big sip. She set down her glass. 'I'll be right back with the nibbles,' she said. 'And then I'll take Rebecca off your hands.'

Paul sniffed. 'Whatever you're cooking, it smells too good to be true.'

'Yankee pot roast.' Margie smiled. 'It's an old family favourite. I was raised by a grandma who was too old-fashioned not to trust red meat.'

Rebecca made unhappy noises and began kicking her feet, but Paul laid her across his lap and gave her his finger to play with.

'I know what you mean,' he said. 'I try to cut down, but there are some things you just can't resist.'

'You can't resist these,' Trisha said, setting a plate of mushrooms on the coffee table. 'Here, let me take her.' She reached for the baby and sat down with her on the carpet. 'You're good with babies, you know that, Lieutenant? It's a talent not a lot of men have.'

Paul did not answer.

Margie cut in. 'Trisha, that was Rob on the phone. He wanted me to tell you that he's coming out here. He'll arrive about noon tomorrow.'

She watched her sister-in-law brush the baby's hair back without saying a word.

'That's a good sign, Trish,' Margie said softly. 'He misses you and Rebecca. He's decided he's ready to make the next move. Maybe he's ready to open up.'

Trisha nodded, but she seemed subdued. 'Rebecca needs changing,' she said. 'I might as well feed her and put her down for a nap so we can have dinner in peace.'

Paul stood up when Trisha did and watched her leave the room. 'She's a gem,' he said, easing back in his seat. 'I hope it works out well for her.'

'Yes,' Margie said, passing the mushrooms. 'Here. Try one of these.'

146

He ate it with gusto. 'Perfect,' he said. 'Another family recipe?'

'Nope,' Margie shook her head. 'Grandma trusted red meat, all right, but she wasn't too sure about mushrooms.'

He smiled and looked at her, and Margie felt sure he could hear her heart beating. She tried to think of something witty to say, but her mouth seemed suddenly dry.

'So,' he said, breaking the silence. 'Tell me, what's with Glenn Walters?'

Margie considered. 'He's a bright kid, explosive and manipulative, and totally lacking in remorse. He sees the world from his own perspective—a classic psychopathic personality.'

'Insane?'

'No. He perceives reality except as it pertains to his behaviour.'

'A potential killer.'

'Maybe,' Margie said. 'But so far, he's only killed an animal. If his lawyer has his way, he'll be out on the streets before you can say Sigmund Freud.'

Paul grimaced. 'Can't say I'm surprised. I see it happen all the time. We lock up a menace and the court kicks him loose to prey on his next victim....'

Margie met the lieutenant's gaze. Neither said a word, but each knew the other was thinking of the brutal murder next door.

Emma Danziger was out of sorts when she signed in Sunday afternoon. It hadn't seemed like any big deal when Rosalie asked her to trade shifts, but now she wished she were home with the newspapers and her feet propped up on the chaise instead of giving up her steady day off so Rosalie could go to a party.

'When will I ever learn?' she muttered, writing her name with a flourish. 'Good old Emma, always happy to do a friend a favour, even if it means I work till eleven and come right back in the morning.'

'Careful, Emma, you're talking to yourself.' Lilly Platz leaned on the counter. 'You know what they say, when you start answering, then you know you're in trouble.'

Emma frowned. 'Very funny. You're a real comedian, you know? Just brief me, will you, so I can get on with it and you can take yourself home.'

'Touchy, touchy,' Lilly said. 'But I bet I can make your day. You know the creep in 6114? The one you said was so sneaky? Well, Dr Hammer discharged him yesterday. Bye-bye, Mr Kiefer.'

'Humph,' said Emma. 'Good riddance. He was a mongrel, that one.' She picked up a chart. 'What else is new? Is Clancy mobile yet?'

In ten minutes, Emma was updated. 'So

go home,' she told Lilly, bending down to put her purse under the counter.

'Oh,' Lilly said. 'That's another thing. Ferguson hit the ceiling this morning. No more personal belongings are to be kept at the nurses' station. Everything is to go to the locker room.'

Emma sighed and retrieved her purse. 'Like she's got nothing better to do. Well, if you're going down there, do me a favour and stow this for me, will you?'

'Sure.' Lilly took the bulky red bag and slung it over her shoulder. 'I'll put it in my locker. The combination's twelve-four-three. Don't work too hard. See you tomorrow.'

The only good thing about Sunday afternoon, as far as Emma was concerned, was that so many visitors were on the floor that the patients needed less from the nurses. By seven fifteen, when her dinner break came, she was surprised to find she wasn't half-tired. Taking a key from a nail on the wall, she went to get her purse from Lilly's locker.

She could tell the minute she entered the locker room that something wasn't right. There were several doors standing wide open, and sweaters and other stuff lay on the floor.

A few of the nurses never bothered to lock up their personal belongings. They

149

figured as long as the room was locked, that was all they needed to know. Maybe now they would change their minds. Emma bent to pick up a lipstick. She was sure someone had been in the locker room going through other people's things.

Closing the door firmly behind her, Emma looked down the hall. She saw Dr Pfennig, still in a scrub suit, just going into his office.

'Dr Pfennig!' she called, running after him, knocking on the door. 'It's Emma Danziger, Dr Pfennig. Someone's rifled the nurses' locker room!'

She waited, but there was no response. She knocked loudly again. She heard a muffled sound. 'Dr Pfennig, are you in there? Please, I need your help!'

The door opened and Emma rushed in. 'Dr Pfennig? Doctor, where are you—'

By the time she saw her attacker's face, she was no longer able to scream.

CHAPTER 14

Monday morning was crisp and sun-washed, a perfect fall morning, and Margie made the drive to the hospital feeling better than she had in weeks.

Her dinner party had been a great success, and Rob's decision to come to California was one that filled her with optimism. To boot, she thought she had established a breakthrough with Glenn Walters when she'd seen him in his cell on Saturday, and she was looking forward to talking to him again after making a few calls to Arizona.

She pulled into her assigned parking area and walked the distance to the hospital entrance with a decided spring in her step, but she knew immediately that something was wrong when she stepped into the lobby.

It was far less crowded than usual, and steeped in a sort of hush. Two police officers were conferring by radio in front of the bank of elevators.

She had to show her identification before she could take the elevator, but when she asked the officers what was going on, they told her only that security was being tightened. Frowning, she took the elevator to eleven and crossed to the forensics unit. Mack's expression was grave as he buzzed her in.

'What's going on?' Margie asked.

'Trouble on six.' His tone was confidential. 'It seems a nurse was killed. A doctor discovered her body in his office sometime yesterday evening.'

Margie felt her body go slack. 'Who? Do they know who did it?'

The guard rubbed his ruddy face. 'Her name was Danziger, Emma Danziger. If they have a suspect, they're not saying. There's nobody in custody that I know of. But the cops have been all over the building ever since last night.'

Margie nodded. 'I'll be in my office. I have some work to do. Let me know if you hear something, will you? I may be on the phone.'

In her office, she took a deep breath and leaned against her desk. Two murders in four days, both very close to home—one where she lived and one where she worked. Coincidence? Margie shuddered.

Her gaze travelled to a spiral-bound directory at the far end of her desk, the listing of professional forensic psychologists, put out by the licensing board. She reached for it, looked at the blue paper cover, and flipped through the pages for her name.

The incongruity of the board's thinking was something that had always bothered her. They designated parking areas out of sight of the prisoners, insisted on using the title Mrs, and requested unlisted telephone numbers in local directories if you lived in the area where you worked. Yet this book, intended as professional reference, was available in any library where anybody—even a former patient released from prison—could find it without any difficulty.

She read the listing under her own name: Reed, Marjorie R, her professional degrees, her home address, and the name of the hospital where she worked.

She sat slowly, the book in her hand, trying hard to be reasonable. But she began to think about former patients who might have decided to look for her; ex-convicts, perhaps, who might have convinced themselves that her testimony had sent them to prison. Was one of them toying with her, trying to frighten her by preying on people around her?

Margie closed her eyes and tried to visualize again what she had seen, or not seen, in the stairwell on the night she'd run out there like a blooming idiot after hearing Jeanne Kerns scream.

Was there something she'd missed, a shadow, anything? She shook her head. No. But she couldn't shake the feeling that she, as well as Trisha and the baby, might be in more danger than she had realized.

She sighed. In the four years she'd been working with criminals, she had worked with hundreds of patients; most of them in the Connecticut system, but a fair number in California. Could she possibly hope to remember them all? To guess who might hate her enough to kill?

She debated calling Paul Sellers. She could run the theory by him. But he would be busy if he were involved in the investigation of the nurse's death downstairs. Anyway, after yesterday afternoon, Margie knew she would be seeing him again.

She smiled despite herself, abashed to realize how right Trisha had been; it seemed her interest in Lieutenant Sellers was more than just professional.

But this was not the time to think about it. Or about the murders, either. Trying hard to put it all out of mind, she found the notes she'd left for herself on Friday and dialled Scottsdale, Arizona.

The young surgeon who'd found Danziger's body was slight and prematurely balding, earnest and cooperative, but with little to add to what he'd told officers the night before. He'd come in to make rounds and found his office door unlocked and Emma's still-warm body on the floor.

'I wish there was something more I could tell you,' Carl Pfennig said. 'I liked Emma Danziger. She was a crusty old broad, but she kept things humming up here. I'll miss her. We all will. And I hope you find the son of a bitch who killed her.'

Paul Sellers nodded. 'I hope so, too. Thanks. You know where to reach me.'

The sixth-floor corridor was nearly empty and so hushed he could hear the squeak of his soles on the ancient, polished floor. A few patients had been moved to other floors, the nursing supervisor had told him, but for the most part the staff who came on duty this morning had had to swallow their collective shock and get on with the business at hand.

The supervisor, Miss Ferguson, rose to meet him. She was a plump, pleasant-looking black woman. 'Lieutenant, here's the list you wanted of the things that were missing from the nurses' locker room. It's mostly cash, small amounts, no credit cards or anything like that.'

Sellers nodded, scanning the list. 'There was a nurse you thought I might talk to.'

'Yes,' she told him. 'Lilly Platz. She was on duty last night. She was probably Emma's closest friend. She called in sick today. I can give you her number, if you want to call her.' She began flipping through a Rolodex.

Sellers waited while she wrote down the number.

'Is there anything else, Lieutenant?'

'No. Thank you. Not at the moment.' He reached for one of his cards. 'I'd appreciate a call if you hear something, though, or anything someone may have seen or heard.'

He hesitated at the bank of elevators, tempted to make a floor-by-floor search in case the guys last night had missed something. But they'd told him they'd been over every inch, even the deserted twelfth floor. He had to assume they'd done their job. There was nothing more to do here now.

Sheriff's Investigator Ellen Romaine was barely five feet three, a slim, sloe-eyed feather of a woman who looked like anything but a cop. But she was bright and efficient, one of the most efficient at the Santa Clarita station. Paul Sellers meant it when he told her he was happy to have her on his team.

'I guess this is as good a time as any,' he said, 'to bring you up to date.' He withdrew some photos and reports from a drawer and spread them across the desk. 'This is Kerns.' He pointed to a photo. 'Killed late Wednesday, early Thursday. This is Danziger, the nurse who was killed last night. Here, have a look.'

Ellen looked at the photos first, then scanned the initial reports. 'Bludgeoned, both of them. Blunt force trauma. You're thinking there's a tie-in?'

Sellers shrugged. 'A possibility. The

156

crimes were two miles apart. Get something out on the teletype, will you? M.O, victims, everything.'

'Right away,' Ellen said. 'What about prints, samples?'

'Prints from the Kerns place should be here now. I'll run them through this morning. It'll be a few hours, anyway, before we know what they turned up over at the hospital.'

'Okay.' Ellen stood. 'I've got a report to finish. Then I'm clear. I'll get on the teletype. Look out, Santa Clarita Basher.'

'Basher.' Sellers chuckled to himself, knowing that the name would stick, especially if some hotshot reporter ever got it on the record.

CHAPTER 15

Detective Ray Nance strode into his office and stared, baffled, at his desk. The biggest floral arrangement he'd ever seen was parked squarely in the middle of it.

'Hey, hey, lover boy,' a young, female voice carolled from behind him. 'You must have done something special this weekend. These just came about an hour ago.'

Nance glowered at the administrative

clerk. 'Yeah, well thanks. See ya later.'

The girl backed out and Nance circled the desk, looking at the flowers in amazement. He hardly knew one bloom from another and he'd never gotten flowers in his life, but he knew enough to be pretty sure that whoever had sent these had spent a fortune.

Finally, he plucked out a tiny envelope and pulled a card from inside.

It may not be the Garden of Eden,
but our love will continue to bloom.
I will love you always, and never less
than on the seventeenth of June.
—Susie.

Nance stared at it, grinning foolishly, a prickling at the back of his eyes. He knew if he stared at it too much longer, he was going to have to cry. He stuffed it into his shirt pocket and sat behind the desk.

He was about to call Susie when he noticed the phone messages littering the scarred desktop. He scanned them quickly, discarding a couple, sorting the rest into piles. At the bottom was a message from Joseph Landesmann, Vejar State Hospital. He plucked it out, picked up the telephone, and dialled the direct number.

'Dr Landesmann speaking.'

The voice was gruff, but Nance felt

158

lucky to find him in. 'Ray Nance,' he said, 'Santa Barbara P.D. You left a message for me Friday.'

'Yes, Nance, I wanted to let you know I've determined a couple of things—the name of the patient you may be looking for, for one thing—Kiefer, Dennis Kiefer. A transient, treated for gastroenteritis. Discharged September twenty-third. He said something about going up to Oregon, I think to work in a lumber camp. I believe I may have written the address of a temporary shelter for him on the back of one of my cards.'

Nance paused. *September 23. The day the gardener was killed.* 'Kiefer, spell it.'

'K-i-e-f-e-r, Dennis, with a double *n.* Twenty-four, tall, thin, sort of blondish, as I recall, with a scruff of beard and some facial pitting, scars from teenage acne.'

'Good stuff, Doc. Oregon, you said?'

'That's what he told me, yes. And there's something else you may be interested in. He's been in this hospital before, several times, as a matter of fact, each time with gastric distress. I've asked for hospital reimbursement records, since the state foots the bill for emergency care of transients. I thought you might find them helpful.'

'You're all right, Dr Joseph Landesmann. I appreciate your being on top of it.' Nance hesitated. 'Let me ask you something. I

159

guess I'm asking your opinion. Was there anything about this transient, Kiefer, to indicate he might have been violent?'

It was the doctor's turn to pause a moment. When he spoke, his voice was low. 'On September twenty-first, he had to be restrained from physically attacking a nurse.'

By the time Margie got off the phone, she was dying for a cup of coffee. But she'd managed to scrawl four pages of notes that filled in a lot of gaps, and she knew she had cleared a major hurdle in her readiness to assess Glenn Walters.

She swung her purse over her shoulder and stepped next door to Chet's office. The blond psychologist was dictating a report. Margie wiggled her fingers in silence.

'Hi.' Chet smiled, turning off the machine. 'I stopped in before, but you were busy.'

'Wanna cup of coffee?'

'Sure,' he said. 'Hang on, I'll be right with you.'

He made a few notes, slipped on his jacket, and took Margie's arm. 'You heard about what happened on six last night,' he said, leading her down the hall.

Margie nodded as Mack buzzed them out. 'Yes. My God, what a shock. Mack told me a doctor found her.'

160

'Pfennig, Carl Pfennig, a neurologist, I heard.' Chet held the elevator door. 'I don't know him, but I don't think it matters. He's not a suspect or anything. He just had the misfortune of finding her in his office when he came in to make rounds.'

Margie grimaced as they rounded the corner into the cafeteria. 'Mack doesn't think there *is* a suspect. That's what's hard to believe. How do you kill someone in a busy hospital and just walk quietly out?'

Chet shrugged, drawing two coffees from an ancient steel urn and setting them on a tray. 'Damn, I could sure use a cheese Danish.'

'That's what you always say.'

'I know, and one of these days I'll remember to stop at Harry's on the way to work.'

He looked sceptically at a jelly doughnut. 'Want one of these?'

'Thanks, no.'

'Anyway, apparently that's what happened.' Chet led the way to a table. 'The nurse had gone on a dinner break. Nobody saw or heard anything. By the time she was found and the cops came in, the killer was long gone. I hear they scoured the place, stem to stern. Who knows what they might have come up with?'

They sat at a window seat, sipping

coffee. Margie had little to say, deciding there was probably nothing to be gained by confiding her fears to Chet.

'So how was your weekend?' He asked her finally.

'Nice. Oh, it was nice.' She felt a tiny stab of guilt at not having asked Chet to dinner. He was a friend, a good friend, and Margie felt that somehow she'd betrayed him. But she knew now, beyond a doubt, that there could be no more between them, and it might have been an uncomfortable afternoon if he'd been there along with Paul Sellers.

'I was able to talk to Trisha,' she said. 'Sort of get a feel for what's happened. And Rob, my brother, is flying in today. I'll know more when I talk to him.'

It occurred to her than that Chet's primary field had been in family counselling. He'd talked more than once about leaving forensics to hang up a private shingle again.

'Chet,' she said, 'I was just thinking. If Rob and Trisha need help, if they want counselling, I'm much too close to get involved professionally....'

Chet nodded, pushing up his glasses. 'I'm honoured if you're thinking of me. If there's anything I can do, I'd be glad to try. Is it anything you want to talk about?'

'No,' Margie said. 'Not now, anyway.

Let me talk to them first. But I want you to know I'd feel perfectly confident sending them to you.'

Chet looked as though she'd handed him a gift, but what she had said was true. 'Listen,' she said. 'There *is* something I'd like to talk about, if you have another few minutes. Glenn Walters. I've just spent an hour and a half talking to people in Scottsdale.'

'Sure,' Chet said, getting up to refill their Styrofoam cups. 'Was he an axe murderer or a cocaine junkie before he came to the Golden State?'

Margie smiled. 'Neither, actually. But there's quite a juvenile history. From what the school people tell me, I would say he's exhibited sociopathic tendencies since he got to Scottsdale when he was twelve.'

'Violent?'

'Yes.' Margie nodded. 'But not in a traditional sense. A lot of vandalism, suspected arson, a felony gun theft two years ago. And he was given to scaring the pants off people with some truly bizarre behaviour—once he painted his face with war paint and ran after some kids with a hatchet.'

Chet whistled. 'Quite a rap sheet. All as a juvenile, huh?'

'Yes, and although it was never proven, it's possible he's killed animals before.

163

There are several people in the Scottsdale area whose pets mysteriously disappeared. I spoke to three who believe unequivocably that Glenn Walters killed them.'

'So the cat in the mailbox wasn't a first.'

'Yes and no,' Margie said. 'This was the first time he brought the carcass back and left it for the owner to find.'

Chet drained his coffee cup. 'It would seem your patient is getting increasingly bold. Makes you wonder how long it will be before he starts cutting up people.'

Margie repeated the story Paul Sellers had told her, which she had checked out with the butcher and the market manager. 'Here was this kid,' she said. 'Utterly calm, stabbing sides of beef with an ice pick.'

Chet shook his head. 'So what do you think?'

'I think he's clearly dangerous. I think he's emotionally and behaviourally disordered and criminally responsible for his act. But he has a glib attorney, who'll make every attempt to trivialize the charges and cut him loose.'

She was reminded briefly of Roy Gates, but she shook the image away.

'Happens all the time. You know that,' Chet said. 'But there is another wild card. If the pet owner who suffered the heart attack dies, Glenn may be charged with manslaughter.'

164

'I know.' Margie sighed. 'It's sad to think that a woman may have to die before Glenn can be ordered to seek psychiatric help instead of wiggling through the cracks in the system.'

Chet got up. 'What about his family?'

'Not much help, I'm afraid. Passive mother with a lot of guilt and a stepdad I can't get a handle on.' Margie followed Chet to the elevator. 'And I'm still waiting for records from Arizona.'

The elevator doors opened on eleven. 'So what's next?' Chet asked.

'I'll confront Glenn with what I know about his past and see if there's something I've missed—a shred of remorse, anything to indicate a concept of moral reality.'

'Anything new downstairs?' Chet asked as Mack buzzed them in.

'Not that I've heard,' the guard replied. 'The place is still crawling with cops, but you know the longer it takes them to score, the colder the trail will get.'

Chet headed down the hall to his office. 'Duty calls,' he said. 'I should have dictated this report last Friday, but better late than never.'

Margie turned to Mack. 'Would you call back, please, and tell them I want to see Walters?'

The guard blinked. 'Glenn Walters? Didn't anybody tell you?'

165

'Tell me what?'

'Walters is gone.'

Margie stared. 'Gone where?'

'Couldn't tell you. All I know is, he was released to his attorney yesterday.'

In a far corner of the hospital cafeteria, blue eyes watched her coolly, studying her back as she drank her coffee with a blond guy wearing glasses.

She was dark-haired, small, and slim, just the way he remembered. He thought it was her, but he wasn't sure. He would have to see her face again—the pixielike face with the big dark eyes and the little upturned nose.

She worked here, all right, that much he knew. He had seen the ID badge on her dress. He spooned up the last of his ice cream and thought about getting some more.

CHAPTER 16

Margie stood at the window of her office, thinking she might as well go home. She was caught up on paper work, anxious to see her brother, and disinclined to wait around for Glenn's attorney to return her call.

She glanced at her watch. Four o'clock. She would give it one more try. If Carlton Richards was not in his office, she would pack it in for the day.

'This is Margie Reed,' she told the secretary. 'Is Mr Richards in?'

The secretary's voice had an imperious air. 'Mr Richards has received your message. He's expected in the office at any moment. I will tell him you called again.'

'Thank you. I don't expect to be at the hospital more than just another few minutes. If he doesn't reach me this afternoon, ask him to try tomorrow.'

She straightened her desk with short, quick movements, annoyed not because Richards had moved his client to a private psychiatric facility, but because he'd not shown her the professional courtesy of telling her he was going to do so.

Well, she told herself, buttoning her grey plaid jacket and reaching for her purse, like it or not, her responsibility in the case was probably coming to an end.

In a way she was sorry. She believed Glenn Walters was seriously disturbed, and she hoped the psychologist hired by the family would do a thorough assessment. She decided she would submit her own assessment to the court, with a copy to the new psychologist.

She was halfway down the hall when she heard her phone ring. She wavered, then retraced her steps.

'Hello,' she said, assuming it was Richards. 'This is Margie Reed.'

Instead it was a woman's voice, low and controlled, on the other end of the line. 'Hello,' she said. 'This is Phyllis Hardesty. Anna Hardesty's daughter.'

Anna Hardesty, Margie knew, was the owner of the cat Glenn had mutilated. But she hadn't known the woman had a daughter. 'Hello,' she said. 'How is your mother?'

Phyllis Hardesty paused. 'The same, I guess. No one seems to want to venture a guess as to whether or not she'll recover. But I need to talk to you about Glenn Walters. There are some things you ought to know.'

Margie hesitated. She could tell Phyllis Hardesty that Glenn was no longer her patient. But then, until she had confirmation, she supposed that, technically, he was.

'I was on my way out when you called,' she said. 'Is it something can wait until tomorrow?'

'Of course. Whenever it's convenient for you. I'll be happy to come to the hospital.'

Margie set the appointment for eleven

168

in the morning and left the office quickly, eager to get home to her own apartment and talk to Trisha and Rob.

Walking briskly through the parking lot, she rummaged for her keys and then groaned, standing rooted to the spot, when she saw that her tyre was flat.

'Damn,' she muttered, moving closer and bending to have a look. The afternoon had begun to darken and the Honda was deep in shadow, but the left front tyre was flat, all right. It was going to have to be changed.

She thought for a minute. She could change it herself. It wouldn't be the first time, but the idea of changing it on the blacktop, in her stockings, decidedly lacked appeal.

Sighing, she made her way back to the hospital, to the bank of telephones in the lobby.

'This is Margie Reed,' she told the Auto Club dispatcher, giving her membership number. 'My Honda is parked in the employees' lot at Santa Clarita State Hospital. I must have picked up a nail in my tyre. It's flat and I need it changed.'

It seemed like ages before she saw the familiar blue-and-white tow truck, but when she looked at her watch she was surprised to see that less than fifteen minutes had passed.

'Lucky, at that,' she muttered to herself, waving the driver toward her car.

The driver was a middle-aged, barrel-chested man with a steady stream of chatter, but he worked quickly, Margie noted with relief as she waited in the near-darkness.

'Kind of deserted out here, isn't it?' he asked her as he worked. 'Bad place for a woman to be parked, out here all alone.'

'No choice,' Margie told him. 'It's an assigned parking area. It isn't very well lighted, either, but I try to be out before dark.'

He tossed the deflated tyre aside and began to mount the spare. 'Probably picked up a nail or a rock,' he told her. 'You wanna be sure and get it fixed. Let's just get this baby on and then we'll have a look.'

Margie waited while he tightened the lug nuts and reached for the discarded tyre.

'Uh-oh,' he said, hauling himself up. 'I'm afraid you're gonna need a new one.' He held it out for Margie to see. 'This one's been slashed pretty bad.'

'I've got good news and bad news,' Paul Sellers said as Ellen Romaine sat down.

'Tell me the good news first,' she said.

'Sure.' He leaned back in his chair. 'The good news is the prints from Kerns's apartment are great—clear as a bell.'

Ellen nodded. 'So the bad news is there are no such prints in the computer.'

'That's part of it.' The lieutenant stood up. 'It never ceases to amaze me. Six million prints on file in the system, and we end up looking for a guy who's not only never been busted, he's never even applied for a driver's licence!'

'Well, it happens,' Ellen said. 'But you said that's only part of it.'

'Right. It gets worse. If it is the same guy, he got smarter when he got to the hospital. There were no prints in the nurses' locker room that don't belong to the nurses—or in the office where Danziger was killed. Makes it tough to establish a tie-in.'

Ellen shrugged. 'Maybe, maybe not. We'll see what else turns up. I sent crime scene scenarios out on the teletype up and down the state.'

'Good.' The lieutenant put on his jacket. 'Call it a day if you want. I'm on my way to see a friend of Danziger's. It's practically on my way home.'

Lilly Platz's condominium was more than a little out of his way. But she'd been on shift the night Danziger was murdered and she'd readily agreed to see him, so he put off dinner and headed south to San Fernando Road.

The condos were squat, little grey-brown

boxes, each identical to the next, but he found the number easily enough and waited while the doorbell chimed.

The woman who answered was mid-fiftyish, small, round, and dishevelled. She was wrapped in a bathrobe and her eyes were red-rimmed, as though she had been crying. 'You must be the lieutenant,' she said, before he could produce his credentials. 'Come in, come in.' She led him inside and pointed to a small, flowered sofa.

He sat, leaning forward as she sat across from him in a green upholstered rocker, but before he could say anything she began to cry and drew a wad of tissues from her pocket.

'I'm so sorry,' she murmured, dabbing at her eyes. 'I haven't been able to stop. Ever since we found poor Emma, I'm afraid I've just been beside myself...'

'I understand,' Paul told her gently. 'Emma Danziger was your friend.'

Lilly nodded, blowing her nose. 'I've known her for years and years. We worked together. I was so happy when she transferred up to my floor! I just—I can't believe she's gone! And in such an awful way—'

He waited while she wiped fresh tears from her already puffy eyes. 'I know,' he said. 'We'll find her killer. That's why I

172

wanted to talk to you.'

Lilly took a deep, shuddering breath. 'Lieutenant, there's something I want to tell you. You may think I'm crazy or something, but I think—I know who might have done it.'

Paul looked at her. 'Who?' he asked. 'Someone you saw that night?'

Lilly shook her head. 'That—homeless person. He knew Emma didn't trust him. He was discharged earlier, but he must have come back. Maybe she found him in the locker room.'

Paul frowned. 'A homeless person. Someone you knew at the hospital?'

'A patient,' Lilly said, balling up the tissues. 'He was a patient and then he was discharged. Kiefer was his name. Dennis Kiefer. He knew Emma didn't trust him.'

'Kiefer,' Paul said. 'A patient on your floor? When was the last time you saw him?'

Lilly grimaced. 'Saturday morning. That's when he was discharged. But he could have come back. He knew where everything was, the nurses' locker room and everything. What if he came back and got in the locker room and that's when Emma saw him? What if he killed her when she caught him stealing and then dragged her into the doctor's office?'

Paul asked her to start from the

173

beginning, from the first time she saw Dennis Kiefer. He took out his notepad and began to write, though he knew he would remember what she said. By the time she was finished, he had somewhere to start. Maybe the best shot he had.

He was still mulling over what she had told him as he turned onto Valencia, vaguely aware that he was getting hungry and that he didn't feel like eating alone. On impulse, he pulled into the nearest gas station and dialled Margie Reed.

'Hi,' he said, somewhat cheered when she answered on the first ring. 'Paul Sellers. I wanted to thank you for that fabulous dinner yesterday. And if you'll forgive me for the short notice, I'd like to return the favour.'

'You're welcome,' she said, hesitating a beat. 'Really, it was my pleasure. But if you mean tonight I'm not so sure. My brother's just arrived from Connecticut.'

He could have kicked himself. 'Right, of course. I'm sorry, I guess I forgot. Well, listen, I—'

'Wait,' Margie cut in. He heard her talking to someone else. In a moment she was back. 'Paul,' she said. 'I'd be very happy to join you.'

Now he was puzzled. 'I'm in the neighbourhood. I could be there in ten minutes.'

'Great,' she said. 'See you then.' He heard the call disconnect.

When he pulled up ten minutes later, she was waiting in front of the apartment complex, looking wonderful in a red print dress that set off her dark eyes and hair.

'You must think I'm really daffy,' she told him, getting into the Buick. 'I adore Rob and I'm dying to talk to him, but I think they want some time to talk alone. To tell you the truth, after the first few minutes, I began to feel like an intruder.'

Paul said nothing.

'And anyway,' she said. 'I'm glad to have the chance to talk. I've been wondering about some things, ever since the murders. I'd like to get your reaction.'

'At your service,' Paul said drily, pulling out of the driveway.

Margie looked at his unsmiling profile and suddenly wanted to kick herself. 'Paul,' she said. 'I'm so sorry. I'm saying this all wrong. I've made it seem as if I accepted your invitation purely because it was convenient...'

He smiled at her briefly as he eased into traffic. 'Well. Is that the way it is?'

'No, the fact is'—her voice was nearly a whisper—'I wanted to be here.'

Denny took the stairs to the twelfth floor

of the hospital, then paused at the stairwell door. He listened, and when he was sure it was clear, he pushed the door ajar.

He was certain the cops had cleared out of the building, but there wasn't any point in taking chances. When he heard nothing and saw no lights, he let himself in quietly, anxious to get out of the surgical scrub suit he'd been wearing since yesterday afternoon.

It had worked perfectly. Denny smiled to himself. He could go anywhere he wanted now. Dressed in the scrubs, with the paper hairnet on his head and paper shoes on his feet, he looked like any other surgical orderly anywhere in the building.

He would have to snatch an ID badge to pin on the pocket of the scrub shirt since he'd heard the cops bitching about sloppy security when they were searching floor by floor. As if it mattered. By the time the cops got there after somebody found the nurse, a hundred people could have come and gone right through the main entrance.

Denny stripped to his underwear, folded the scrub clothes, and stretched out flat on a mattress. He closed his eyes. Everything was fine. He was doing it all just right. Cops or no cops, he was too smart. He had everything under control...

CHAPTER 17

The restaurant Paul chose was woodsy and intimate, like the little dinner houses she remembered back East, and Margie sank onto the leather banquette grateful for the chance to relax.

'You look like a woman who could use a glass of wine,' Paul told her as he ordered a bottle of white zinfandel and a tray of crab puff appetizers.

She laughed. 'You're right. It's been a rotten day. I feel like my nerves are frazzled.'

She wanted to tell him about the slashed tyre, which had first angered, then alarmed her. But she had nearly ruined the evening once already. She decided to bide her time.

'I'm glad you came tonight,' Paul said. 'I wanted to be able to say "thank you." For yesterday, I mean. It was a wonderful day. I really had a good time.'

Margie smiled. 'We enjoyed it, too. Trisha said you fit in like family. She couldn't get over how well you handled the baby. You must be the oldest of ten!'

Paul seemed to waver. 'No,' he said.

'Actually I'm the younger of two. But I've had a little practice. With babies, I mean. I—used to have a son.'

Margie could have kicked herself. 'I'm sorry—' she started to say.

Paul stopped her. 'No, it's okay. Jamie would have been eight. He was killed four years ago, he and my wife—by a drunken driver on the freeway.'

Margie looked up. 'Oh, Paul, you don't have to—'

'No, please. I want to tell you.' His voice was gentle. 'See, it's always stood like a barrier, like a ghost, between me and—other people. I wanted you to know, to break the barrier down, so we can—get to know each other better.'

Margie was silent, looking at her hands, crossed on the tablecloth in front of her.

Paul put one of his hands over hers. 'I'm sorry. That sounds like I'm rushing you. Maybe you haven't the slightest desire to know me better except as Lieutenant Sellers.'

Margie looked up. 'That isn't so.' *Oh, God, this was going to sound maudlin!* 'Paul, my fiancé, was killed last Christmas, in Connecticut, during a grocery store robbery. I know all about those barriers you mentioned. I've battled my share of ghosts.'

The waiter appeared to pour the wine

and present them with oversize menus. By the time they ordered and the waiter had gone, they had lapsed into awkward silence.

Then Paul smiled crookedly, raising his glass. 'To ghosts that may someday stop haunting.'

Margie nodded, trying to smile. 'I'll drink to that,' she said.

The food was excellent, a wonderful sea bass surrounded by bouquets of vegetables. Margie, finding herself suddenly starving, ate until she thought she would burst.

When they were finished, she looked at Paul and settled back against her seat. 'I don't believe I did that,' she said. 'I am totally, absolutely stuffed.'

'Good,' he told her, looking pleased as he signalled the waiter for coffee. When it was poured, he leaned forward. 'Now it's time for business.'

'Business?' Margie was genuinely puzzled.

He gave her a bemused smile. 'Something was bothering you when I called you this evening. You told me so yourself. So now you've been patient long enough. Tell me what's on your mind.'

The anxiety Margie had felt earlier had somehow lost its urgency, and she wondered now if her imagination had simply run away with her. But she trusted Paul, who would surely tell her

179

if he thought she was way off base. She forced herself to marshal her thoughts and find a way to begin.

'Paul,' she said. 'When I left the hospital tonight, I found one of my tyres had been slashed. It's not a big deal, it happens, I know, even in public parking lots. But a couple of other things have happened, too, since the night Jeanne Kerns was killed. When I put them all together, I begin to wonder if someone is trying to tell me something.'

She told him about the funeral flowers that had been delivered to her apartment and the dead bird she'd found on her doorstep.

'I didn't think much about them at the time,' she said. 'But now they seem almost—ominous. Most frightening of all is the simple fact that two murders have already occurred: one where I live and one where I work. It seems somehow more than coincidental.'

Paul nodded. 'Maybe,' he said. 'You think someone's trying to scare you? Maybe the someone who watched you from the stairwell the night Jeanne Kerns was killed?'

Margie sighed. 'I know it sounds unlikely. But yes, Paul, that's what I think.'

He listened quietly as she told him her

fears that it might be a former patient, who'd transferred his hatred of society to her and managed to track her down.

'Maybe I'm verging on paranoia,' she finished. 'But there, I've said it, anyway.'

Paul leaned forward and looked directly at her. 'You're not verging on paranoia. At this point, I'm not ruling anything out. Any idea who it might be?'

Margie shook her head. 'That's the hard part. I've worked with hundreds of patients. Any number of them could have taken it into their heads that it was I who put them behind bars.'

'That's not good enough,' Paul told her. 'Go through every file, if you have to. Give me a list that's anywhere near manageable and we'll start checking current whereabouts.'

It was nearly eleven by the time they'd finished and Paul walked her to her door.

'Thanks for dinner,' she told him, fishing for her keys. 'It was wonderful. Just what I needed. And thanks for listening to my half-baked theories. I feel a little better already.'

'Tomorrow, as soon as you get a chance, get started with that list. Even if it turns out to be a dead end, we'll both feel better for having tried it.'

Margie studied him. 'I don't know why, but there's something so calming about you. You make me feel safe. Silly, almost for being frightened in the first place...'

A slow smile softened his features. 'That's the nicest thing I've heard all day. But don't get cocky. Lock your door—'

'... And don't take candy from strangers.'

His gaze met hers and she laughed, embarrassed. 'Sorry. Didn't mean to be flip.'

He nodded. 'Sleep well. I'll call you tomorrow.'

'Yes. You, too. Good night.'

She listened as his footsteps faded in the stairwell, then let herself into the apartment. The lights were off, but the television was on and she could see the outline of her brother's form silhouetted in the glow.

'It's me, Rob,' she said quietly, locking the door behind her.

'Hi,' he said. 'Did you have a good time?'

'Yes. Has Trisha gone to bed?'

'She's an early bird. I guess she has to be, getting up to nurse the baby. I thought I'd wait up so we could talk awhile—that is, if you're not too tired.'

She *was* tired, Margie realized, stepping out of her shoes. But she also wanted to talk to Rob. 'I've got an idea,' she said. 'Why don't you make us some hot tea while I get out of these clothes?'

Quietly, not wanting to wake Trisha or Rebecca, she tiptoed into the bedroom, got out of her clothes without turning on a light, and groped for her nightgown and robe. By then, her eyes had adjusted to the darkness and she peered into the closet, selecting a dress and gathering up some underthings she knew she would need in the morning.

She took them to the living room, laid them across a chair, and turned a lamp on low, then turned off the television set as Rob came in balancing two steaming mugs.

'Put them down,' she told him, pointing to the coffee table. 'And then come give me a hug. A big hug. Rob, you can't imagine how happy I am to see you.'

He grinned as he gathered her into a bear hug and held her close for a moment, then laid his chin on top of her head in a well-remembered gesture. 'Remember when we were little and Grandma warned you that you'd better be nice to your little brother, because someday he was apt to be bigger than you and pay you back for every punch?'

Margie smiled, drawing back. 'Oh, yes, I remember. Good thing I listened. You were bigger than me by the time you were ten years old!'

He was taller than Margie by nearly a

foot, with the same dark colouring, but he was thinner than she remembered and his boyish face had developed angles and planes.

'Six months,' she murmured, sitting on the sofa and reaching for her tea. 'It seems so much longer than that since I saw you. How did you get so thin?'

'I don't know.' He shrugged. 'Busy, I guess. No time for regular meals.'

'Trisha's a great cook.'

'Yeah, she is.'

'But I guess you haven't been home much...'

He reached for his tea and sat down across from her. 'You look great, Marg, you really do. Like you're really happy. Happy with your life. Even a boyfriend, huh?'

Margie smiled. 'Not really a boyfriend. You know about what happened next door?'

Rob nodded. 'Trisha told me.'

'Paul is the investigating officer. Part of the reason I saw him tonight was to give him some information.'

'But you do like him. Trisha said—'

'Yes. I do like him. If I have the chance, I'll go out with him again. Beyond that, I don't know...'

Rob looked at her. 'You still miss Frank.'

'Of course I do. I loved him. But I know he would want me to get on with my life, and that's what I'm trying to do.' She saw her brother's jaw tighten. 'You still miss him, too.'

Rob nodded. 'I keep thinking how different it could have been...'

'If Frank had lived?'

'If—I don't know. Lots of things, I guess...'

Margie swirled the tea in her mug. 'You've never been able to talk about it.'

'They never caught him. You know that, don't you? They've never caught Frank's killer.'

Margie said nothing.

'I saw him, Marg. That night in the mountain store. I saw him. His face is burned into my brain. I'll never forget it. Never.'

Rob's voice broke and Margie looked up to see his face contorted, tears welling in the steady brown eyes she'd loved so well since childhood.

'Oh, Rob,' she murmured, putting down her mug and reaching for her brother. 'Talk to me, Rob. Let it out. Please, don't let it destroy you.'

Rob clung to her the way he had when he was just a little boy, the way he had after their mother died and Daddy had left them at Grandma's house in Connecticut.

'Why did they leave us, Margie!' little Rob had sobbed, his eyes enormous in his face.

Margie had held him, as she held him now, speaking softly in his ear, telling him they were going to be just fine, that Grandma loved them very much.

Margie had been nine, five years older than Rob, but she felt older than her years, having long ago come to grips with their mother's long illness and their father's inability to cope.

And they *had* been fine, she and Rob both, with a grandmother who loved them fiercely—who lavished them with hugs and meted out their scoldings with the same easy grace.

'Some things never change, huh, Marg?' Rob said, pulling away and smiling wanly. 'Little Robby takes a fall and comes crying to his sister.'

Margie smiled back. 'Ah, but they do change. Wait till you see my bill!'

Rob chuckled. 'My sister the shrink. Why am I not surprised? You could zap me open and see inside my head for as far back as I can remember.'

'Oh, Rob, I never could. I just loved you, that's all. I could never stand to see you hurt. I still can't, even now.'

Rob made a wry face. 'Good grief, you think something's wrong?'

186

'Be serious, Rob. Whatever it is, it's tearing you apart. It's destroying your marriage and cheating your child, the same way our father cheated us.'

Rob's face sobered. 'That's hitting below the belt.'

'I'm calling it the way I see it. You need help. I can't give it to you, but I do know someone who can try.'

'Another shrink.'

Margie nodded. 'He's good. He's someone you can trust. His name's Chet Anderson. He works at the hospital. He's already agreed to see you.'

Rob got up. 'Little pushy, weren't you? Talking to him before I even got here? What did you tell him, that I'm some kind of nut case who can't control his life?'

Margie kept her voice steady. 'I told him I thought you needed help.'

'Great. Just great. So I spill my guts and he tells you all about it.'

'Please, Rob, you know better than that. What you tell him is confidential.'

'Mmm...' He paced the tiny living room. 'Confidential. Right.'

Margie picked up the empty mugs. 'Rob, I didn't mean to be pushy. If I overstepped my bounds, I apologize. I just hate to see you so unhappy, and Trisha, too. She loves you, you know that, and she doesn't know what to do...'

'It doesn't have anything to do with Trisha. I love her. I love the baby...'

'Then do something, Rob, or you're going to lose them.'

He walked over to the window. His voice was low. 'Call your friend. Find out when he can see me.'

CHAPTER 18

It was after nine when Paul Sellers parked his unmarked Ford and slipped in through the back door of the station. It was more than an hour past his normal arrival time, but he told himself he had the comp time coming after all the overtime he'd put in.

The fact was, he'd slept better last night than he had in a long time, and he'd felt an almost gleeful satisfaction in punching down the snooze alarm button three times in succession before he got out of bed. Then he'd taken a long, lazy shower, slugged down a big tumbler of orange juice, and finished the entire *New York Times* crossword puzzle before he thought about getting dressed.

Now he drew a cup of coffee from the urn in the duty room and took it to his desk, but he'd barely managed the first scalding sip when Ellen tapped on his open door.

'Good afternoon, Lieutenant,' she said grinning, and eased into a chair. 'Heavy date last night or what? I nearly called you at home.'

He blew on the coffee. 'M.Y.O.B. What was so important?'

'Not sure,' she told him. 'Maybe nothing. Then again, maybe yes. Those scenarios I sent out over the wire? Guy called from Santa Barbara this morning. Nance, his name is, Sergeant Nance, Santa Barbara P.D.'

Sellers ventured a sip. The coffee was almost drinkable. 'What did he have to say?'

'He's investigating a ten-day-old murder —a gardener at Vejar State Hospital. The man was bashed over the head with his own shovel while he was tending the posies. Possible suspect is a young white male who'd just been released from the hospital.'

Sellers looked at her. 'Dennis Kiefer?'

Ellen cocked her head.

'Call me psychic.'

She narrowed her eyes. 'Okay, how'd you know?'

'I talked to Lilly Platz last night, a co-worker of Danziger's at Santa Clarita. She flat out told me she suspected this

189

Kiefer. He'd been a patient there, too. He was discharged Saturday, some twenty-four hours before Emma Danziger was killed.'

'Well, well, well.' Ellen leaned back. 'When was Kiefer admitted? Before or after the stewardess thing?'

'Platz was a little vague. I'm going back over to the hospital this morning.' He took a swig of coffee. 'I assume this Nance ran a make on Kiefer.'

'Yeah. There was no rap sheet. But he said he's expecting some state records that could shed a little more light. He's hoping to have them by this afternoon. You can check with him after lunch.'

Sellers nodded. 'While I'm gone, run Kiefer through the moniker file. Also, check with L.A.P.D—'

'Lieutenant, I'm way ahead of you.'

'Right.' He finished the last of the coffee and gave her a rueful smile.

'No problem.' Ellen stood. 'I'll have it by the time you get back.'

Phyllis Hardesty was slim and graceful, with a curly mop of reddish hair and a redhead's creamy complexion. She looked at Margie with bright blue eyes, but dark smudges on the pale skin beneath them suggested sleepless nights.

'Thank you for making time to see me,

190

Mrs Reed. I know I should have called sooner.'

Margie did not bother to clarify her marital status. 'I'm glad you called when you did. I didn't know Mrs Hardesty had a daughter, but I'm eager to hear what you have to say.'

Phyllis shifted her weight in the chair. 'I promised Mother I'd keep quiet. She has a soft spot in her heart for Glenn. Even after he began to harass her, she wouldn't let me call the police.'

'Are you saying Glenn had harassed her previously? Before he killed her cat?'

'I think so, yes, although it was a while before my mother realized it. Then she began to notice odd little things like clean laundry yanked off her clothesline, and roses snapped off the bushes. Once she found a rotting chicken carcass in a bag on her front porch.'

Margie thought briefly about her slashed tyre, the funeral wreath, the dead bird. She forced herself to put it out of mind and focus on the interview with Phyllis. 'Did your mother ever see Glenn doing these things?' she asked.

'Not at first, no. But then, one day, she was walking home from Gelson's Market and she saw him in her front yard. She called out and he ran off, but he began to lurk around the house. He'd hide out

191

of sight if he thought she was watching, but she saw him several times. She thought if she ignored the pranks, he would work up the courage to come and knock on her door.'

'She knew him from the market?'

'Oh, long before. I'm sorry, I thought you knew. My mother was the Walters' housekeeper in Scottsdale until she moved out here.'

Margie raised her eyebrows. 'I didn't know. I don't think the police knew, either.'

'She worked for them for nearly five years. She's known Glenn since he was twelve.'

'I see,' Margie said. 'Nobody in Scottsdale seems to know much about the family. Mr Walters told me he was injured in the mines and that he bought the house in Scottsdale out of his settlement.'

Phyllis smiled. 'That's what he told people, so they wouldn't wonder why he didn't work. But Mrs Walters told my mother there never was any accident. The company paid him to keep his mouth shut. Hush money, she called it.'

'Hush money.'

Phyllis shrugged. 'Some sort of blackmail, I guess. Mr Walters found out his boss at the mine was sleeping with the owner's daughter, who was only sixteen.

She'd meet him at night, apparently, and use her father's office. Anyway, one night Mr Walters had Glenn climb into the offices through a transom and snap some embarrassing pictures.'

Margie stopped her. 'Glenn took pictures?'

'That's what Mrs Walters said. Her husband used the pictures to blackmail the owner. They paid him and made him leave town. She told Mother they had put some money in trust for Glenn and used the rest to buy the house.'

Margie considered. That would explain the money Glenn said he was waiting for. 'You said your mother had a soft spot for Glenn. Why did she leave Arizona?'

'It's a long story,' Phyllis said. 'Glenn was a hard boy to manage. But my mother had raised four boys herself, and she thought she could straighten him out. I think, in a way, she really loved him, even after he started getting into trouble. Do you know about that? The trouble in Scottsdale?'

'Yes, I think so,' Margie said. 'I spoke to the school authorities and the local police and I think I've pieced most of it together.'

Phyllis nodded. 'Well, neither of his parents paid much attention to Glenn, so he and my mother were pretty close. She tried her best, but as things got worse, she felt she was just too old to cope. The Walterses owed her money, and while she was heartbroken about Glenn, she decided to move out here where I live.'

'I see,' Margie said. 'When was that?'

'I guess about a year and a half ago.'

'And the Walterses followed about six months later,' Margie mused aloud.

'Yes,' Phyllis said. 'Apparently, the money ran out, and the house went into foreclosure. And with Glenn having so many weirdo problems, they just packed up and left. Maybe they came here because Mother had written what a pretty place it was. She knew they'd moved, but she didn't know where, until Glenn started coming around.'

Margie nodded. 'But once Glenn was harassing her, why did she keep it to herself?'

'She thought—I don't know. She thought she could help him. She wanted him to trust her.' Phyllis began to cry. 'She's very stubborn...very loyal. She thought...she wanted to help...'

Margie handed Phyllis a tissue and waited until the tears subsided. 'I know how hard this is,' she said at last. 'Why did you finally decide to call me?'

A shuddering sigh. 'My mother was wrong. She couldn't possibly have helped. He's a sick boy—full of venom and spite. A very twisted boy.'

194

'Lunchtime, Margie, if you—oh, excuse me. The door was open. Sorry.'

Chet Anderson stood in the doorway, looking somewhat abashed.

Margie stood up. 'It's okay, Chet. Come in. This is Phyllis Hardesty, Anna Hardesty's daughter. She came in to talk to me about Glenn. Phyllis Hardesty, this is Chet Anderson, another psychologist here.'

Phyllis stood and extended her hand. 'It's nice to meet you, Mr Anderson. Or is it Dr Anderson?'

'Chet will do. It's nice to meet you, too. How's your mother? Margie's told me what happened.'

'No change, I'm afraid,' Phyllis told him. 'It's good of you to ask.'

'Well, listen, I'm sorry I interrupted...'

Margie realized that Chet's gaze had never left Phyllis's face. 'Chet,' she said. 'We're just about finished. Thanks for thinking about lunch, but I really have a ton of work. Maybe Phyllis would like to join you.'

Chet looked at Margie and back at Phyllis. 'Oh. Well, if you're sure. The food's not great here, but it's handy if you're hungry.'

'I'm starved,' Phyllis said, looking at her watch. 'And I'll have to get back to my office, but there's time for a sandwich. I'd love to join you. Thanks. Thanks very much.'

Margie handed her a pad and pencil. 'Just leave your number, Phyllis. Then I can reach you if something comes up. Of course, I wish your mother the best.'

Phyllis wrote her name and number. 'Thank you. Thanks for seeing me.'

Margie watched them leave and made a mental note to talk to Chet later about her brother. Then she went to the file cabinet, retrieved some folders, and sat down at her desk.

Denny hit the button, watched the double doors swing open, and sauntered into the third-floor surgical wing with an air of bored authority.

It was hard to keep from smiling to himself, he was so good at what he did. But he kept the bored expression on his face in case anyone saw him.

It was quiet on the ward, as he expected it would be at this hour of the day. Most of the morning's surgeries were completed, and messy supply carts lined the corridor, waiting for orderlies who had already gone to lunch.

Denny grabbed a cart and moved it slowly down the length of the corridor, whistling softly and checking to see which of the surgeries were still occupied. Only two, he saw, and from the hum of conversation behind each door, he could tell they were a ways from finishing. Good. That was fine. Couldn't be better. He moved toward the end of the corridor.

Peering casually through double glass windows, he saw that the scrub room was empty. He backed the door open, wheeled in the cart, and scanned the room slowly.

A few white coats and a couple of stethoscopes hung from a row of pegs. Denny took a stethoscope, hung it around his neck, and selected a couple of name tags. He glanced toward the door, pinned one of the tags on his scrub shirt, and continued across the room.

There were four watches on a stainless steel shelf directly above the sinks: a Movado, a Piaget, an old Seiko, and one whose name he didn't recognize. He slipped the Movado into his pocket, loaded some wet towels onto the cart, and headed out the door. Then he wheeled the cart to the double doors, hit the button till they swung open and stepped briskly out of the wing.

It was only when the elevator door closed behind him that he allowed himself to smile, nodding pleasantly at the two old men who shared the ride upstairs.

The watch would bring a pretty penny when he got around to hocking it. Now he was hungry. He got off on the tenth floor and headed for the cafeteria.

CHAPTER 19

It was well after one and Margie was starving when she finally put down her pen. As Paul had suggested, she was going through her files, trying to focus on former patients who might possibly want to harm her. She'd made a list of a dozen 'possibles'—including Roy Gates. But the more she persisted, the more she wondered if she was wasting her time—and Paul's.

The funeral wreath she had found at her door, the poor, dead bird on her doorstep...*were* they warnings, like the morbid clues Glenn Walters had left for Anna Hardesty? Or misunderstandings, mere coincidences she was blowing out of proportion?

Even if what she feared was true, if a patient had managed to find her, was it likely he was lunatic enough to kill innocent people just to frighten her? And if he was, would she recognize such lunacy from reviewing her cryptic case notes?

She pushed her chair back, tired and hungry. She was going to get some lunch. Then she would spend the rest of the day dictating her report on Glenn Walters.

The cafeteria was still crowded, but Margie avoided the line, settling for some yogurt and a carton of milk from a row of self-service machines. She walked quickly toward an unoccupied table at the far end of the room and nearly collided with a young man in surgical scrubs approaching with a loaded tray.

'Sorry,' she said, managing a smile. 'That'll teach me to go full tilt. If you don't mind sharing, I don't either. I won't be long in any case.'

He stared at her and seemed to hesitate. He glanced around the room. Then he set his tray on the table and sat without saying a word.

Margie sat, unfolded a napkin, and lifted the lid from her yogurt. 'The least I can do is introduce myself, since I almost knocked you down. Margie Reed. I'm a state psychologist. I work upstairs on eleven.'

He mumbled something she didn't catch and dug into a dish of pasta, one of a number of assorted dishes piled haphazardly on his tray.

She glanced at his name tag. Ira

Jablonsky. She guessed he was a surgical intern. Only an intern could eat like that. She started on her yogurt.

She watched him finish the last of his pasta and start on a dish of cole slaw. Then he buttered a slab of cornbread and downed it in four huge bites.

Margie smiled, sipping her milk. 'Carbo loading, eh? I guess they keep you pretty busy.'

'Yeah, right, they do.' He stacked his empty dishes together and reached for a wedge of pie.

Clearly, Dr Jablonsky's appetite was keener than his social skills. Excusing herself, Margie bused her tray and headed back to her office.

Ray Nance whistled softly and dropped the printout on his desk.

Assuming the state statistics were correct, Dennis Kiefer had been admitted for treatment fourteen times at nine state and county hospitals during the past nineteen months. In addition, he'd been an intermittent or drop-in patient at four neighbourhood health centres.

Nance drummed his fingers on the desk and shook his head slowly. The twenty-four-year-old transient with no next of kin had appeared out of nowhere, traversed the state, and managed to receive more than

$17,000 in medical services without ever reporting an address.

To boot, as far as Nance could determine, Kiefer had never applied for aid, never been arrested, never registered to vote or for the draft. Incredible as it seemed, there were no ready sources of photographs, fingerprints, or descriptions. Apart from what Dr Landesmann had told him, they might as well be looking for a ghost.

Of course, the sergeant told himself, he could request information from each of the facilities that had treated Kiefer. That would take time, and there were no guarantees that anyone else would remember him. But it was a place to start, and Nance had a feeling he would find the gardener's killer.

He had just gotten up to go find a map when Sellers called from Santa Clarita.

'Sergeant,' the sheriff's lieutenant told him, 'I'm interested in hearing what you have. Your Dennis Kiefer checked into Santa Clarita State Hospital hours after a flight attendant was killed here, and checked out less than twenty-four hours before a nurse was found with her skull crushed.'

Nance felt the familiar rush that accompanied every chase. 'Well, well,' he told Sellers. 'Let me FAX you some information. There's a state printout that traces Kiefer's whereabouts through hospitals up and down the state.'

'Up and down the state.'

'You got it, Sellers. The guy has been around. Either he has a bleeding ulcer as big as Oklahoma, or he's crying wolf and bilking the state of thousands in phoney benefits.'

Sellers paused. 'Okay,' he said. 'So we keep this under wraps. Alert the hospitals, give him some slack, and see where he turns up next.'

'Sounds good to me.' Ray Nance nodded. 'And I have another idea. Why don't you take a look at this printout? Then we'll talk again.'

Trisha set the baby carrier down facing away from the sun, then settled herself in a yellow deck chair overlooking the swimming pool.

'Isn't this pretty?' she asked Rebecca. 'Imagine, we're into October! At home, we'd be starting to lay in the firewood, but here they swim all year long!'

Rebecca grinned her toothless grin. 'Gaaa, gaa,' she said.

Trisha laughed. 'I know, I know. It's nice to be outdoors. We'll stay here till Daddy gets back from the store. Then we'll go upstairs and have some lunch.'

From where Trisha sat she could see the hills, and the sun felt warm on her face. She was happier than she could remember being since the day Rebecca was born.

Rob seemed to be making an effort to be more like his old self; he was concerned about her, enjoying the baby, even making plans.

'I can sell houses as easily in California as I can in Connecticut,' he'd told her. 'If you like it here, there isn't a thing to keep us from moving out here permanently.'

Trisha liked it a lot out here. She liked being close to Margie. Most of all, if Rob could be happy, she would be happy too.

Rebecca was sleeping, her fine, long lashes fanned across her cheeks. Trisha smiled, rolled up her jeans, and tilted her face to the sun.

She had no idea how long she'd been drowsing when she came awake with a start. But her heart was pounding and she felt a chill, though the sun was high in the sky.

She looked around frantically, scraping her chair back. Rebecca was sound asleep. Weak with relief, she picked up the carrier and walked across the decking to the gate.

There was no one there, but the gate was open. Had she closed it when she came in earlier? She scanned the courtyard, listened for footsteps. Nothing. Nothing at all.

Rebecca had awakened when she'd swooped her up and now she began to cry. Trisha put her cheek to the baby's. 'It's okay. Just a bad, bad dream.'

But she climbed the stairs to Margie's apartment with a feeling something was wrong.

CHAPTER 20

Margie found two messages on her desk when she came back from lunch. One was an invitation from staff services to a meeting Friday evening. The other was from Carlton Richards, Glenn Walters's attorney.

The invitation, Margie knew, was tantamount to a command. Grimacing, she tucked it into her calendar and dialled Richards's number. To her surprise, her call was put right through.

'Miss Reed.' She recognized the attorney's booming voice and patronizing undertone. 'My sincerest apologies for not getting back to you sooner. I assume you were calling about Glenn Walters.'

'Yes,' she told him. 'Apparently you got the court's permission to move him after all. I thought I'd ask where he is and how he's doing.'

'Well, it's nothing to bother yourself about, Miss Reed. We've got it all under control. I happened to play golf with Judge Wendell on Saturday, and we chatted along the back nine.'

Margie kept her voice even. 'I see. And what did you chat about?'

'Judge Wendell agreed to the private assessment, as long as the family would pay for it, and in view of the DA's change of position, it seemed the most expedient thing to do.'

'Change of position.'

'Well, of course, you wouldn't have heard.' Richards's voice grew confidential. 'As I've said right along, this whole darn thing's been blown way out of proportion. The DA saw that; he's a reasonable man. He's willing to drop the felony charge if Glenn will plead guilty to malicious mischief, and that's just fine with us.'

A misdemeanour, Margie thought. Glenn would probably draw probation—and very likely flee the jurisdiction, even if counselling were ordered.

'I should tell you, Mr Richards, I plan to go ahead and submit a report to the court. Judge Wendell and the DA should have all the information at hand before a disposition is made.'

The attorney chuckled. 'Well, now, Miss Reed. You can save yourself the trouble. The judge has agreed to see us on Monday and consider Mason Eldridge's assessment.'

Margie had never heard of Mason Eldridge, but it wouldn't have mattered if she had. 'No trouble at all,' she told Carlton Richards. 'I've already done most of the groundwork.'

Richards sighed. 'Suit yourself, Miss Reed. Most women do, anyway.'

He hung up without another word and Margie shook her head, reminding herself that men like Richards were quickly becoming extinct. Then, curious about Mason Eldridge, she walked down the hall to Chet's office.

He was seated at his desk, staring forlornly at an ecru-coloured note, the same invitation to Friday night's meeting that Margie had just received.

'An invitation to boredom,' Chet said. 'God, I hate these things.'

Margie smiled. 'Suppose I give you a legitimate reason not to go.'

'Give it a whirl.' He tilted his chair back and motioned for Margie to sit.

'My brother Rob,' she said, sitting. 'He's finally agreed to see you. Suppose I bring him up here Friday night while I get bored for both of us.'

Chet smiled. 'Sounds good to me. And not just because of the meeting. I'm looking forward to meeting Rob. I hope I'll be able to help.'

'I know,' Margie said. 'So! Are you busy?'

'Never too busy for you. Did you ever eat lunch?'

'Sort of.' She shrugged. 'How was your lunch with Phyllis?'

Chet smiled. 'Great,' he said. 'I like her. She's very bright.'

'Also gorgeous,' Margie teased. 'But then I guess you noticed. Listen, I came in to ask a question. Do you know a shrink named Mason Eldridge?'

'Mostly from the newspapers,' Chet said. 'He rarely practices anymore. He seems to be making a tidy living giving expert testimony in court.'

'Meaning he can be bought?'

'I don't know.' Chet shrugged. 'But I have to say it wouldn't surprise me.'

Margie frowned. 'Great,' she said. 'He's doing the assessment on Glenn Walters. If he agrees with Richards that Glenn is harmless, the DA will drop the felony. Glenn will plead guilty to a misdemeanour and never even go to trial.'

'So he'll get probation,' Chet told her. 'Maybe the judge will order him into counselling.'

Margie shook her head. 'He'll run,' she said. 'He's told me that himself. The court should know that, along with his history and the facts leading up to the crime.'

'You're going ahead with your own report.'

'Yes,' Margie told him. 'I'm going to find a juvenile court judge who'll subpoena Glenn's records from Arizona. But even if they shouldn't get here in time, I've learned a lot on my own.'

'Good luck,' Chet said. 'I've already told you, Richards is a power to be reckoned with.'

'Maybe.' Margie got up and moved toward the door. 'But he won't steamroller me.'

She ducked into her office to retrieve her purse, then headed down the hall. 'I'll be back in an hour,' she told Mack as he buzzed her through the heavy outer door.

It seemed to take forever for the elevator to get there and an age before she reached the main floor. But it was a short drive over to the courthouse, and nearly three in the afternoon. With any luck at all, she'd find a juvenile court judge winding up the afternoon docket.

She had walked halfway across the parking lot when the eeriest feeling came over her. She thought she was being followed and stopped and turned around,

208

but there was no one behind her.

Her gaze travelled between the rows of parked cars and swept up the side of the building. But she saw nothing and the windows were blank. She shrugged and continued toward her car.

'This Kiefer's either a walking shadow or the luckiest guy who ever lived.'

Ellen Romaine sat across from Sellers, waving a sheaf of papers. 'I haven't turned up a rap sheet anywhere, or proof he ever existed, except, of course, in those state reimbursement files and all those hospital records.'

Sellers looked up from the map on his desk. 'So now we'll try something else. Come on over and take a look at this.' He moved his chair to make room.

'I've marked this map to show every hospital where Kiefer's been known to be a patient and entered the dates of each confinement according to the state's records.'

'You want me to check for unsolved crimes that correspond with those dates and areas.'

Sellers smiled. 'I love a bright cop.'

'So how come I get stuck with the scut work?'

'It's all scut work, at this point,' Sellers told her. 'What do you think I'm doing?

Contacting every hospital from here to San Diego to alert them in case Kiefer turns up.'

Ellen nodded. 'Okay, okay. I guess there isn't much else we *can* do. I'll start looking for unsolved crimes. It'll come in handy if we find him.'

'When, Romaine,' Sellers said. 'It'll come in handy *when* we find him. Kiefer's found a clever way to keep himself off the streets. What he doesn't know is that we're on to his scam. He's going to lead us right to him.'

He rolled up the map, handed it to Ellen, and gave her a thumbs up as she left. Then he turned back to the list he'd been working from for the better part of the afternoon.

He was concentrating on hospitals and clinics closest to Santa Clarita, assuming that if Margie's suspicions were correct that Kiefer was still in the area. He tried not to focus on what bothered him most—that Margie might well be in danger.

If Kiefer had seen her from the top of the stairwell the night he killed Jeanne Kerns and seen her again during the couple of days he'd spent at Santa Clarita State Hospital, then he knew where she lived, and he knew where she worked. He could get to her at any time. That's what he was telling her by slashing her tyres and

210

planting dead birds on her doorstep.

In fact, Sellers realized, there were two main factors working in Margie's favour: Her brother and sister-in-law were with her at home, and she worked behind locked and guarded doors in the forensics unit of the hospital. Maybe Kiefer was having a harder time getting to her than he'd expected. But maybe she needed to be convinced she must not be alone at any time.

On impulse, he dialled the hospital number and asked for Margie's extension. It rang six times and he was ready to hang up when she picked up the phone, breathless.

'Hi,' he said. 'I didn't think you were there. I was just about to give up.'

'Paul!' she said. He could almost see her smile. 'I just got back this minute. I was out persuading a juvenile court judge to subpoena Walters's records from Scottsdale.'

'Any luck?'

'Yes. The only question is whether they'll get here in time. I've got until Friday to complete my reports and get them into court. Hey, guess what?'

'I don't know. What?'

'There's a message here on my desk from Trisha. She's cooking spaghetti and meatballs. She wants me to call our favourite lieutenant and ask him over for dinner.'

'Sounds terrific. So am I invited?'

'Well, I wouldn't want to disappoint the cook. Seven o'clock?'

'I'll bring the wine.'

'Good. We'll see you later. Paul?'

'Yes?'

'Why were you calling?'

'For a dinner invitation. See you later.'

CHAPTER 21

'I feel like a guest in my own house,' Margie said, coming into the kitchen for the third time in less than half an hour.

Trisha looked up from the cucumbers she was slicing. 'That's the whole idea. You just take yourself and your gorgeous purple jumpsuit right back into the living room. It's the least we can do, since we've come along and just barged into your life.'

Margie opened her mouth to protest, but she knew it would do no good. She knew her sister-in-law well enough to recognize that determined look.

The small kitchen smelled warm and homey, heavily scented with garlic and oregano, and Trisha moved between the stove and the salad board with an air of practised ease.

Rebecca gurgled happily from a blanket on the floor, flailing her fat little legs in the air and chewing on a ring of rubber keys. Even Rob looked perfectly content to be slicing a large loaf of French bread.

'If I were you'—he winked at Margie— 'I'd do as I was told. The last guy Trisha threw out of her kitchen bounced all the way to Hartford!'

Trisha took a step to her left and poked an elbow into his ribs, but Margie guessed from the look that passed between them that some of the tension had eased.

She was still smiling when she answered the doorbell. 'Hi!' she said. 'Right on time.'

'Are you kidding? I could smell that spaghetti sauce cooking from the time I turned off the boulevard.'

Paul was wearing a cable knit sweater over a plaid, open-necked shirt. It was the first time Margie had seen him without a jacket and tie on. She thought he looked younger and more relaxed.

'These are for the cook,' he said, handing her a bouquet of mixed fall flowers. 'And here's the wine, a red Bordeaux, and—oh, yes. This is for Rebecca.'

He held up an old-fashioned Raggedy

213

Ann doll, with sewn-on features and a frilly white apron and a mop of red yarn hair.

Margie laughed. 'I had one just like this when I was a little girl! It's nice to know some things don't change, even in the space age. Come, let me introduce you to my brother, and you can give Trisha the flowers.'

The introductions were swift and easy, and Trisha was pleased with the flowers, but she was even more delighted with the Raggedy Ann. 'Look, Rebecca, your very first doll!'

She got down on her knees to show the doll to Rebecca, who promptly stuck its arm in her mouth. 'Gaaa!' she squealed, pronouncing it delicious and smiling gleefully at Paul.

The four of them laughed, which made Rebecca laugh and bounce up and down on her blanket.

'She's tired,' Trisha said. 'But she won't admit it. I guess she can stay up a little longer. Why don't you two relax in the living room? Rob can help me finish up here.'

'If you're sure,' Margie said, knowing it was useless. 'Okay, okay, we're going.'

She backed into the living room, followed by Paul. 'There's no use arguing with Trisha. She's determined that we should be out here courting while she's being mother hen.'

Paul laughed, sitting beside her on the sofa. 'I like her. She has a grip on real life. And I, for one, have no objections to sitting here courting you.'

Hearing him say it made Margie smile. 'What an outmoded word. Courting.'

'I don't know. It seems to suit you. There's something traditional about you. A quaint, honest dependability. Even your name. Marjorie.'

'You can blame my mother for that.' She sighed. 'Her ancestors were Pilgrim stock. I guess you can take the girl out of New England, but you can't take New England out of the girl.'

'Do you mind that?'

She gave him an impish smile. 'Would I rather be quaint than sexy?'

'You're both,' he said. 'Refreshingly quaint. And incredibly sexy.'

Margie could feel the crackle of energy that drew his face to hers, a current so strong that it surprised and unsettled her. She turned her face away.

'It's so soon.' She managed a whisper. 'It makes me feel—unfaithful. You must feel it, too. You told me your wife—'

'Shh...Margie, please.' He cupped his hand under her chin and turned her around to face him. 'Don't ever compare,

215

Margie. Yes, I loved my wife. And it took a long time—it took knowing you—to make me realize that I didn't die with her.'

'But, Frank—'

'I know. You're still grieving. Grief is a lonely thing. But when you're ready to reach for a hand, I hope it's mine you reach for.'

She was still looking into his steady brown eyes when Rob called that dinner was ready, and Paul reached over to touch her cheek and pull her to her feet.

'Will you look at this baby!' Trisha laughed, carrying a basket to the table. 'Poor thing, she's had it. Would you pick her up, Rob, and carry her to the bed?'

Rebecca was sleeping peacefully on her stomach, wrapped around Raggedy Ann, her little bottom up in the air and her chubby legs tucked under her.

'I think she likes her Raggedy,' Margie said as Rob gently scooped Rebecca up and carried her, still holding the doll, down the hall to the bedroom.

'Good,' Paul said, holding a chair out for Margie. 'Every little girl should have a Raggedy. Trisha, if this tastes as good as it smells, it may just have to be outlawed.'

Ray Nance watched Susie go into her apartment building and waited until the light went on in her kitchen and she waved at him from the window. Then he waved back, pulled away from the kerb, and reluctantly headed back to the station.

Susie understood, he knew, that he had to return to work, that a cop's hours weren't always nine to five, and there was nothing to do but accept it. But it bugged him that he'd had to leave her as soon as they finished dinner.

'I've got plenty to do,' she'd told him. 'I'm working on the guest list, and I want to call a couple of caterers. And the realtor will be calling about some new listings if we want to look at houses this weekend.'

He smiled, pleased at how happy Susie was and how lucky he was to have found her. They would have a good life. They would make a good life, he and Susie together.

Brant Stevenson was waiting in the parking lot, carrying a sketch pad and a briefcase.

'Am I late?' Nance asked, leaning across the seat to unlock the passenger door.

'Nope.' The police artist folded his lanky frame into the unmarked Ford. 'Don't care, anyway. I'm on overtime. Hope this gig is worth it.'

'Me, too,' Nance said, checking his notes and heading back into traffic. 'Gotta see the man when we can. I've a feeling

217

it's going to pay off.'

Landesmann's house was small and unpretentious, a grey clapboard bungalow. It sat on a bluff overlooking the ocean on a prime chunk of land, though, an expensive bauble out of the reach of most, even in pricey Santa Barbara.

There was nothing pretentious, either, about the woman who answered the doorbell, wiping her hands on a dishcloth. 'You must be Sergeant Nance.' She smiled, extending a plump, damp hand. 'Come in, come in. We're running a little late, but that's the way it is with a doctor. My husband is expecting you. He's in the den. I was just making some coffee.'

Landesmann, like his wife, was short and round, not at all what Nance had expected. He indicated an over-stuffed sofa.

'Thank you for seeing us,' Nance told him. 'I appreciate your making the time.'

Landesmann sat heavily in a chair across from them. 'I'm not really sure I can help you. As I told you on the phone, my memory of Kiefer is hazy, at best. I see so many patients, you know, and often no more than once or twice before they leave the hospital.'

'I understand that, Dr Landesmann,' Nance said. 'All I want you to do is talk. Try to picture Kiefer as well as you can and Officer Stevenson here will draw what you recall. Sometimes, after a witness sees a sketch, he's amazed at what he does remember.'

'All I remember for certain,' Landesmann began, 'is a long, thin face, and acne scars, deeply pitted. I remember noticing that.'

'What colour was his hair?' Nance prompted.

Landesmann frowned. 'I'm not sure. Blondish, maybe, dishwater blond. Longish, I think it was long...'

'Was it parted?'

Stevenson opened his sketchpad on his lap and drew some preliminary lines.

'I don't recall,' Landesmann said. 'It was sort of—I don't know...lanky. Like it hung over his forehead. He kept brushing it away, brushing it out of his eyes...and that's another thing. He smiled a lot, but he smiled only with his mouth. His eyes were dull. Flat and dull. He didn't smile with his eyes.'

Nance continued to ask questions and Landesmann answered thoughtfully, occasionally glancing at Stevenson's sketches and nodding or shaking his head.

By the time the police artist had the portrait completed, Landesmann was smiling broadly.

'That's it, that's him!' he said. 'Utterly amazing. I never would have believed it.

Now that I see it, there's no question. That is Dennis Kiefer.'

Nance looked over at the finished sketch. 'Dr Landesmann, thanks a million. This will help. It may even tie Kiefer to a couple of murders down in the L.A area.'

He was anxious to go and have the sketch reproduced so he could send copies to Sellers. But Mrs Landesmann insisted they have coffee and homemade apple pie.

'I don't know which are worse off,' she said. 'Doctors or policemen. Too much work and long hours, long, crazy hours...'

Nance nodded, gazing out the window at the waves lapping at the shore. He thought he could have told her, but instead he smiled. 'Great pie, Mrs Landesmann.'

'I hope you don't mind that I suggested the walk.' Paul followed Margie down the stairs.

'Not for a minute,' Margie said. 'I'm so stuffed I can hardly breathe!'

'You have a great family.' He moved beside her. 'You're very lucky to have them.'

'I know. Having them here makes me realize how very much I've missed them.'

Paul was silent for a long minute as they traversed the brick courtyard. Then he said, 'Margie, I'm very glad they're here. Especially now, I mean.'

Margie looked at him.

'I don't mean to alarm you, but this is something I have to say. I think we have a lead on the man who killed Jeanne Kerns, and possibly Emma Danziger. But we don't know where he is, and until we do, I don't want you to be alone.'

Margie kicked at a pile of leaves that were massed around a lamppost. 'Because of what I told you the other night. What I believed were threats...'

'Yes. You told me you were fairly sure you had been observed from the landing right after Kerns was killed. If that's true, we don't want to give the observer an opportunity to get near you.'

Margie thought that over. 'Tell me about this man—this killer you have a lead on.'

'Don't know much yet. We're only starting to gather information. Apparently, he's some sort of transient. We think it's possible he left your apartment building after he killed Kerns and checked himself into Santa Clarita State Hospital. It's a ploy he's used before, in Santa Barbara, and possibly other areas.'

'What about his background, his methods?'

Paul shrugged. 'Too soon. We know that Emma Danziger was killed in much the same way as Kerns, and that Kiefer had just checked out of the hospital the day before Danziger was killed.'

'So both were crimes of opportunity, really, with burglary a possible motive.'

'So it would seem,' Paul agreed. 'We'll have more information tomorrow. Meanwhile, I'm not taking any chances—especially where you're concerned. I mean it when I tell you you're not to be alone, either at home or at the hospital.'

Margie paused in the light of a gas lamp as they headed back toward her building and drew a folded sheet of paper out of her jumpsuit pocket. 'You asked me to make a list,' she began. 'Former patients who might want to frighten me. Do you still want it?'

'Of course,' he said. 'I told you I'd check it out.'

She nodded. 'It's hard. There've been so many. But I did the best I could, based on the nature of the crimes they'd committed and my own assessments of each case.'

He unfolded the paper and scanned it briefly in the circle of diffused light. Then he refolded it, put it in his pocket and turned to look at Margie.

He seemed to be studying her face in the lamplight, and she felt herself drawing closer. But he simply reached out and touched her cheek. 'Come. Let's get you inside.'

A solitary figure watched from the shadows. The guy was a cop, no doubt of it. But that was okay. He would find a way. He would find a way to get to her.

CHAPTER 22

Margie turned off the Dictaphone machine and leaned forward in her chair, checking her notes to be sure she'd covered everything in her report to the court on Glenn Walters.

There was no question he was competent to stand trial. She had wanted to make that clear, despite Carlton Richards's calm assertion that a trial now seemed remote. As for the rest of it, she had focused on material that might otherwise never come to light—including Glenn's relationship with the owner of the dead cat and his history of antisocial behaviour.

Glenn was obsessed with a mother, Margie had written, who deserted him emotionally at a critical time in his development. Glenn acted out his anger by terrorizing others in increasingly bizarre ways.

Unable to cope with a second desertion by the housekeeper and surrogate mother, he had elected to punish Anna Hardesty, first by planning ways to frighten her and finally by killing her cat.

Margie shuddered. This was no boyish prank, as Carlton Richards would have the court and the district attorney believe. Glenn Walters was a budding psychopath with a total lack of remorse. Left on his own, without psychiatric intervention, he would continue to be a danger to society.

Again, she thought of Roy Gates. There was such a startling similarity. She sighed, gathering her notes together and stuffing them into a folder. She had done what she could—in both cases. What happened next was out of her hands.

Ellen Romaine was in Sellers's office before he'd finished his first cup of coffee.

'Romaine,' he said, looking at her face. 'I hope you don't play poker.'

She stifled a grin. 'Very funny. So okay, I'll keep it a secret.'

'Keep what a secret?'

She put down her clipboard and walked to the corner of the cubicle. 'What's this?' she asked, circling twice around a plant as tall as she was.

Paul sipped his coffee. 'It's a plant.'

'I can see that.'

'Okay. It's a philodendron. Does all right in artificial light, doesn't need much water.'

'Uh-huh.' Ellen circled the pot again. 'Did it grow up through the floorboards?'

'No. I carried it in this morning. Got tired of living in a cell.'

A slow smile spread across Ellen's face, but she had the good grace to say nothing.

Paul threw his paper cup into the trash. 'Come on. Whattya got?'

The investigator picked up her clipboard and drew a chair closer to the desk. She nodded at the state map posted on the wall. 'Follow the bouncing ball.'

Picking up a felt-tipped marker, Paul walked over to the map.

'Eureka State Hospital,' Ellen said.

Paul marked an *X* at Eureka.

'Kiefer was admitted June thirteenth, 1988, discharged two days later. At dawn on June thirteenth, according to local authorities, the body of a gas station attendant was found by his boss who was just coming into work. The guy had been bludgeoned to death with a jack and the till had been jimmied open. No suspect ever arrested.'

'Victim's name?'

'Jonas.'

Paul made a note. 'Okay. What else have you got?'

Ellen looked at the clipboard. 'Mendocino County Hospital, Kiefer admitted August sixth—one day after the body of Amy Howard was discovered near the entrance to Fort Bragg. She'd been bludgeoned to death, and her car was found a short time later in a ditch off the main road.'

'No suspect,' Paul muttered, marking the map accordingly.

'Right,' Ellen said. 'Shall I keep going? He begins to crisscross the state.'

The desk sergeant called.

'Fax for me out at the desk,' Sellers said. 'Stay here. I'll be right back.'

When he returned, he tossed the slick white sheets on the desk in front of Ellen. 'It's from Ray Nance in Santa Barbara,' he told her, coming around to look again. 'According to Nance and a reliable witness, you're looking at Dennis Kiefer.'

Together, they studied the narrow, pockmarked face, the listless, deep-set eyes.

'So now what?' Ellen asked.

Paul picked up his marker. 'We'll finish what we're doing here and make a few dozen copies of that drawing. If Lilly Platz at Santa Clarita confirms that's the Kiefer she saw, then we'll split up the list of hospitals and clinics and start taking the drawings around.'

Ellen nodded. 'It's hard to believe that it might be just that simple. Wait for Kiefer to check himself in somewhere, and get out there and bust him.'

Paul grimaced. 'It's not that simple. The trick is to find him first—find him before there's another victim. Before he checks himself in...'

He pictured Margie and his blood ran cold at the thought that something might happen to her. Then he remembered something else, and he reached into his coat pocket and drew out a folded piece of paper.

'I'm not sure there's anything much to this.' He handed the list to Ellen. 'But I want every name on this list checked out, and I want to know their current whereabouts.'

Ellen looked at him. 'Local heroes?'

'Some. A few from Connecticut. If they're incarcerated, I want to know that. If they're not, I want to know where they are.'

'Is it top priority?' Ellen glanced at the list and attached it to her clipboard.

Paul deliberated. 'Probably not. But get it done ASAP... Okay, Bakersfield, October last year. A body was found in an oilfield.'

'Two days after Kiefer was discharged from Kern County Hospital...'

He was getting restless and the money was running low. He was going to need some cash. Denny wondered if he could find a pawnshop within jogging distance of the hospital.

He'd been out before, feeling perfectly safe in his hospital greens and stethoscope. But he hadn't gone that far from the hospital, and now, lying on a mattress in his twelfth-floor hideaway, he weighed the pros and cons. The more he thought about it, the more excited he became about the prospect of carrying it off.

Rummaging around in the murky darkness, he found his cache of watches, selected one, and slipped it into the pocket of his dingy green scrub suit. He debated changing to the T-shirt and jeans he'd pilfered from the doctors' washroom, but he decided there was no point in giving some shop clerk any real clothing to describe.

Not that the clerk would have any reason to describe Denny to anyone. He was too smart to try anything else besides hocking the watch, and a struggling intern hocking a middle-priced watch would not attract attention.

He took the stairs all the way down,

the blood pumping in his veins. He was strong and smart; he would take care of everything and do it in his own sweet time. Breathing deeply of the outside air, he began the jog toward town.

Trisha folded the last of the towels and handed the stack to Rob. 'Bottom shelf, hall closet,' she said. 'And there's one more load in the dryer.'

'I'll get it.' He put the towels away and came back into the living room. 'When the baby wakes up, we can take a walk. It looks like a beautiful day.'

Trisha smiled, pleased at his effort to be helpful and endlessly cheery, though she knew he was bored and a little nervous about seeing a psychologist on Friday.

'Rob,' she said, touching his arm as he walked past her toward the door, 'thank you. For everything, for following me out here and trying to make things better.'

He hugged her to him. 'I love you, Trisha. That's the one thing I know for sure. When you took Rebecca and went away, there was only one thing that mattered—getting you back and making you happy. That's what I'm going to do.'

She wanted to tell him that wasn't all that mattered, that he had to be

229

happy with himself, but Rebecca woke and started to wail. Reluctantly, she let Rob release her.

'Okay, sweet thing,' she cooed at her daughter. 'I guess you've napped long enough. I'll change your diaper while Daddy gets the laundry, and then we'll go for a walk.'

She dressed Rebecca in a yellow playsuit and carried her over to the window, trying to judge whether it was cool enough to put on a sweater, too. She noticed someone at the perimeter of the complex who seemed to be staring up at her. She frowned. That was ridiculous. She turned away to look for the baby's sweater.

He was still standing there when she turned back. She began to feel uneasy, remembering her panic the other day when she'd wakened at the side of the swimming pool.

She moved gratefully into the hall at the sound of Rob's key in the lock. 'Rob? Honey, will you come here a minute?'

He walked in and set down the laundry basket. 'Sure. What's up?'

She went to the window, but the figure had disappeared. Feeling silly, she sat on the bed and scooped up Raggedy Ann. She handed it to Rebecca. 'Nothing,' she said. 'I was looking for the baby's doll...'

CHAPTER 23

'That's him! That's Kiefer,' Lilly Platz announced, tapping a neatly manicured finger on the drawing.

Paul Sellers turned the sketch around so that it faced Olive Ferguson. The nursing supervisor nodded. 'She's right. It is definitely Dennis Kiefer.'

'Okay,' Paul said. 'And this man, Kiefer, was a patient on this floor until the day before Emma Danziger was killed.'

'Absolutely,' Lilly said firmly. 'We can show you the records to prove it. He was a sneaky type, always prowling around, and he knew Emma was keeping tabs on him. He made a big show of saying good-bye to everyone the morning he was discharged. But I'll bet you anything he sneaked back up on Sunday and went after poor, dear Emma.'

Paul looked at Lilly's flushed face. He wanted to believe she was right. He wanted to link Jeanne Kerns's death to Danziger's and link them both neatly to Kiefer. Then he could concentrate on getting Kiefer off the streets, far away from Margie Reed. It wouldn't be easy, with no prints at the hospital and prints that were unidentified from Kerns's apartment.

'I will want copies of Kiefer's chart,' he told the nurses. 'Particularly anything Miss Danziger might have entered to indicate she and Kiefer had clashed.'

Olive Ferguson went to her desk and began to rummage through a drawer. 'I knew there was a reason I keep every scrap of paper anybody hands me around here. Emma wrote me a memo, Lieutenant, I remember that now, the day that Kiefer was admitted. She told me she suspected he'd wandered off the floor and that she thought we'd need to watch him closely.'

There was also the matter of the robbery, Paul realized, as the supervisor sorted through papers. Someone had rifled the nurses' locker room. It could have been Dennis Kiefer, but it could have been anyone, leaving no particular proof that Kiefer had killed Emma Danziger.

'Here it is!' Ferguson exclaimed, handing the memo to Paul. 'See? It's dated September twenty-ninth, the day Dennis Kiefer was admitted.'

Paul read Danziger's cryptic note written in small, neat script, complaining that Kiefer was often out of bed and possibly had managed to leave the floor. *Watch this one*, Emma had written. *This one could give us all a headache!*

'May I have that, Mrs Ferguson?' Paul asked the nurse. 'Along with a copy of Kiefer's chart.'

'I'll have to call it up from Medical Records. I can have it in an hour or so.'

'That's fine,' Paul said. 'I'll be back in an hour. And thank you both for your help.'

Lilly Platz's pudgy face almost seemed to quiver. 'You catch that son of a gun, Lieutenant. He's the one who killed Emma!'

Paul nodded. 'I'm doing my best.'

He hoped Lilly Platz was right.

'Let's tough it out and go for something hot.' Chet led the way through the cafeteria.

'Maybe some soup,' Margie said, following. 'What can they do to ruin that?'

It was early for lunch and the line was short. Chet picked a chicken pot pie. Margie got a bowl of vegetable barley soup, and they carried their trays to a window table.

'Looks like rain.' Chet looked out the window. 'It's darkening up out there.'

Margie looked out at the greying landscape. 'That would almost be a pleasant change. Except that I plan to go over to court this afternoon and hand-deliver my report on Glenn Walters.'

'Finished, eh?'

'Yes.' Margie nodded. 'For whatever good it's going to do, I want to be sure Judge Wendell sees it.'

'Margie.' Chet stood up and waved toward the doorway. 'I think someone's looking for you.'

Paul Sellers waved back and strode across the room. 'They told me downstairs you'd just come up here. Mind if I join you for lunch?'

Margie smiled. 'You told me not to be alone, but I didn't expect a police escort.'

Paul grinned. 'Nothing like that. I'm waiting for some records to be copied. How's the food?'

'Generally lousy,' Chet said. 'Although the pot pie's not all that bad.'

'You know Chet Anderson,' Margie reminded Paul. 'Obviously, Chet remembers you.'

'Of course. Lieutenant Sellers.' Chet offered his hand. 'Go get a tray and join us.'

'Thanks. Don't wait. Your food will get cold. I'll be back in just a minute.'

Margie tried to concentrate on her soup, but she knew that Chet was watching her. 'What?' she asked, looking up finally.

A roguish smile relaxed Chet's face. 'I knew that.'

'What?'

'Lieutenant Sellers. His interest is more than professional. And you lit up like the Las Vegas Strip the minute he walked across the room.'

Margie could feel her face redden.

'Please, Margie, it's great. I saw it that night when he met us at your place. I couldn't be happier for you.'

Margie moved her spoon through her soup. 'Then you knew it before I did. I'm still not sure—'

'Yes, you are. You're just not ready to admit it.'

She looked at Chet. 'You're a good friend. I wish it could have been more.'

'Don't,' he told her. 'It is or it isn't. I hope we'll always be friends.'

The roguish smile returned to his face.

'What?' Margie put down her spoon.

Chet's fork poked holes in the crust of his pie.

Margie paused. 'Phyllis Hardesty?'

He made a show of eating a mouthful.

'Come on, Chet. Friends.'

'Okay, okay. We had dinner last night. I'm seeing her again tonight.'

Margie grinned. 'I could tell you liked her. I did, too. She seems like a lovely person.'

Paul came back to the table and set down his food, a chicken pot pie and a salad. 'Looks like rain,' he said, pulling out a chair.

Chet nodded. 'We were just noticing.'

'We need it,' Margie said. 'But I hope it holds off until after I get back from court.'

'Do you have to go?'

'Yes,' Margie told him. 'I'm waiting for the Walters report to be transcribed. As soon as it's ready, I'm taking it over personally. I want to hand it to Judge Wendell.'

Paul poured dressing from a plastic packet over his spinach salad. 'As soon as I pick up those medical records, I'll be leaving, too. I could run you over to court and run you back. It wouldn't be out of my way.'

Margie gave him a measured look. She knew what he was thinking. If he gave her the ride, it was one less outing she would have to make alone.

'Thanks,' she said softly, not wanting to get into it with Chet sitting at the table. 'But I may be there awhile, talking to the judge. I wouldn't want to hold you up. It's a short drive, and I promise I'll be careful, even if it does rain.'

Chet looked from one to the other of them, as though he sensed an underlying message. 'Well, Lieutenant,' he said finally. 'How's the investigation going?'

Paul seemed to hesitate, chewing his food and taking a long drink of iced tea. 'Fairly well, I think. As a matter of fact, there's something I'd like to show you.'

He pushed his tray away, reached into his coat pocket and brought out a folded sheet of paper. Unfolding it, he placed it on the table so that both Margie and Chet could see it.

'Take a good look at this man,' he told them. 'Have either of you seen him before?'

'No,' Chet said, shaking his head. 'I'm sure I never have.'

Margie looked at the pencil sketch of a youngish-looking man, a long, thin face, an angular nose, hair falling over his forehead.

'No, I don't think so,' she said frowning. 'Although, I'm not sure...'

'Take your time,' Paul told her. 'Go back over the past few days. Imagine the face in different settings—at home, at the hospital, anywhere...'

Margie looked up, surprised to realize Paul was indicating a recent encounter. She had been searching her memory, trying to tie the face with a patient she'd had in the past.

'The past few days...' She faltered, looking down. She studied the sketch again.

Paul was silent, but she felt his scrutiny. It made her uncomfortable. 'I don't think so,' she said. 'No. I really don't think so.'

Paul's gaze searched her face. He seemed about to speak. But then he nodded, folded the sketch and put it back in his pocket.

'Well,' he said brusquely. 'A shot in the dark. Keep the face in mind. If anything comes to you, I want to know about it. I'd want to know right away.'

'Who is he, Lieutenant?' Chet asked.

Again, Paul seemed to hesitate. 'He was a patient here at Santa Clarita from Thursday through Saturday of last week. There's a possibility he may be a suspect in the robbery and murder downstairs.'

Chet pushed his glasses up on his nose. 'But the murder was Sunday,' he said.

'I know.' Paul drained the last of his tea. 'This guy is apparently a transient. But he knows his way around a lot of hospitals up and down the state. We'll be posting his picture in admitting rooms statewide, hoping he'll turn up again. When he does, he may be implicated in several murders over the course of the last few months.'

Is he implicated in the murder of my neighbour, too? Margie wanted to ask. *Is this the man I'm supposed to be avoiding? The man you think has been leaving me messages?*

But Paul was already getting up, picking up his tray, and Margie was not eager to pursue the matter at the risk of alarming Chet. It was bad enough that Paul was ready to restrict her every movement. She didn't want Chet worrying as well, hovering like a mother hen.

As though he sensed her unasked questions, Paul smiled at Margie. 'I'd like to talk a little, later,' he said. 'Any chance I can take you to dinner?'

She did not hesitate. 'Sure,' she said. 'But I'd like to make it early. There are some things I have to do—'

'No problem,' Paul said. 'I can pick you up here at five. We'll leave your car in the lot and I'll bring you back afterward so you can drive it home.'

And you can follow me. Margie smiled. He was determined to keep her in sight. She found it touching. 'Okay,' she said. 'I'll look for you at five.'

CHAPTER 24

By the time Paul picked up Kiefer's medical records from Olive Ferguson and headed downstairs to his car, it had started to sprinkle lightly. But in the two minutes it took him to get out of the hospital parking lot, it had turned to driving rain.

He switched his windshield wipers to high and turned on his headlamps, confounded as always at the sheer ferocity of these early fall California storms.

It was going to be a long night at the station, and at the Highway Patrol office too, as car after car was dispatched to respond to a growing number of traffic accidents. People joked that it was so long between rains that Californians forgot how to drive in them, but the truth was that oil deposits built up on the roads after weeks or months of dry weather, and a sudden rain mixed with the oil made the roads hazardously slick.

Paul realized, as he drove carefully, that he could relax where Margie was concerned. Coming from Connecticut, she was undoubtedly accustomed to negotiating slick, wet roads. And it was unlikely any killer was going to be out after her in this storm.

It was not surprising that Chet had not recognized the face in the drawing he'd shown them earlier. But Paul had hoped that Margie would recognize it, despite the fact that she claimed she saw no one on the night her neighbour was killed. It wouldn't be the first time that a bad fright had played tricks on somebody's memory, and Paul hoped that seeing the drawing might help Margie to remember.

He'd been lucky so far in that the press had not attempted to link Danziger's death to Kerns's. In fact, Paul was forced to admit, there *was* no positive link. But he believed that Kiefer had killed them both, and Margie suspected the link. It was up to him to be sure she was safe until he nailed the bastard.

The station parking lot sat on a slope that rarely bothered anybody, except in the rain, when the runoff collected in a gulley near the back entrance. Turning off the engine and lights, Paul made a run for the door, but he found himself sloshing through three inches of water, soaking his shoes and socks.

He stood in the hallway, shaking the water off his lightweight blue jacket, but he felt damp clear through and his rubber-soled shoes squished loudly on the asphalt tile floor.

'Get caught in Biscailuz Creek?' Ellen asked as he stomped into his office.

Paul had to smile at her reference to the sheriff under whose auspices the station had been built.

'Yeah,' he muttered. 'It's rotten out there. Phones must be ringing off the hook.'

'They are. I'm sitting here counting my

blessings that I'm not on traffic detail.'

'Well, don't get too comfy.' He hung up his jacket. 'We're gonna be right out among 'em. That sketch Nance sent has been positively ID'd as the elusive Dennis Kiefer, who was admitted Thursday to Santa Clarita State Hospital the morning after Kerns was killed—and who, I might add, was discharged Saturday, a day before Danziger bought it.'

Ellen nodded. 'I plotted those graphs you wanted and teletyped out some more inquiries. Oh, and I checked out the names on that list you gave me. It's over there, on your desk.'

Paul sat down and scanned the list of names Margie had given him last night. Next to each name, in sprawling script, Ellen had made a notation; 'incarcerated,' 'paroled,' 'deceased while in custody,' 'present whereabouts unknown.'

He made a mental note to inquire further into the whereabouts of those who were unaccounted for, though he had to admit it would be more to appease Margie than because he believed it was pertinent. It seemed to Paul that when he caught Kiefer, the threat to Margie would be eliminated.

'Thanks,' he said, pocketing the note. 'I promise, no more scut work. I spoke to admitting at Santa Clarita and left a sketch of Kiefer, and I'll be right out there getting drenched along with you while we take sketches to the other hospitals.'

Ellen groaned. 'That's what the fax was invented for. Not to mention the telephone.'

'No doubt,' he told her. 'We'll be using them both for facilities out of the area. But I want us to establish face-to-face contact with every hospital within a fifty-mile radius. I'd be willing to bet Kiefer's within that range, and I want that sucker fast.'

Ellen looked forlornly through the water-spattered window into the driving rain.

'Tell you what,' Paul said. 'Get out that list of hospitals we had and mark the ones within our radius. I'll go find us some slickers and caps and a couple of cups of coffee...'

Margie signed the top copy of her report on Glenn Walters and stuffed it into an old leather briefcase.

The torrential rain had taken everyone by surprise, and she did not have a raincoat, but she did keep a battered red umbrella in the bottom drawer of her desk for just such emergencies as this. Tucking it under her arm along with her briefcase, she buttoned the jacket of her tweed suit, slung her shoulder bag over one shoulder, and headed down the hall.

243

'If anyone needs me, I'll be in Judge Wendell's court,' she told Mack as he buzzed her out. 'I expect I'll be back in an hour or so. If not, send a rowboat and a search party.'

She had meant it as a joke, but standing at the top of the hospital steps and watching the rain sluice down in heavy sheets from the overhang, she debated whether the trip was really necessary.

Of course it *was* necessary if she wanted to be sure that her report reached Judge Wendell before Monday's informal hearing. Bracing herself, her bag and briefcase held tightly under her arm, she bent low under the flimsy umbrella for the long trek to her car.

Her shoes and stockings were soaked and the hem of her skirt was darkened with moisture by the time she slid into the Honda. But Margie felt a strange and breathless exhilaration. It was refreshing to be dealing with real weather for a change, even if she was not properly prepared for it.

She drove the two miles to the courthouse slowly, negotiating the roads and the flooded intersections with practised if near-forgotten ease. Parking in the visitors' area, she made the short run into the building without getting too much wetter, and she managed to smooth her hair and jacket on the way to Judge Wendell's chambers.

She had expected to talk to the court clerk, but the outer office was empty, and to her surprise, the judge called to her from his chambers as she debated what to do next.

'Ms Reed,' he bellowed. 'Come in, come in, I assume you're looking for me.'

Nathan Wendell had always seemed to Margie the quintessential magistrate: tall and ascetic-looking with a ruddy complexion and a haughty nose under a thatch of silver-white hair. He looked at her now with a hint of amusement in his flinty blue eyes. 'Only a woman with a sense of purpose would be out on a day like this, Ms Reed. Would I be far wrong if I guessed you are delivering your report on young Glenn Walters?'

Margie felt the corners of her own mouth turn up. 'No, Your Honour, you wouldn't. Mr Richards informed me you had agreed to hear them informally Monday morning. I thought perhaps I might have more information than Mr Eldridge has had time to gather.'

Imposing even from the bench, Judge Wendell towered over Margie. For a long moment, he rocked on his heels. Then he motioned her to a chair.

'I'm not a coffee drinker, but I have some hot tea. You look like you could do with a cup. Tut, tut, no buts, how do you like it, milk, sugar, lemon?'

Margie hesitated. 'Lemon, please. But I—'

'Upp! I told you, no buts. It's no trouble. It's the least I can offer you when you've made this trip in a downpour.'

She watched him pour tea from an enamelled carafe into delicate china cups, adding milk to one and using silver tongs to place a lemon wedge on one saucer.

'There,' he said, placing her cup on one corner of his massive mahogany desk. 'Just pull your chair up and enjoy your tea while we have this little chat.'

The black leather chair she sat in was heavy, but she managed to move it forward a few inches. 'Thank you, Your Honour, that's very kind. I must admit it smells wonderful.'

The judge settled back in his wing-backed chair and took a sip of his tea. 'I take it you don't hold Mason Eldridge in particularly high regard.'

Margie blinked. 'It isn't that, Your Honour. I've never even met him. It's just that he hasn't had much time. He only received the case last Monday.'

The judge did not appear to have heard her. 'You're quite right in your opinion. Mr Eldridge appears to spend more time in court than he does in the practice of psychology. It did not endear me to Mr Richards's cause that his client had elected to engage him.'

'But Mr Richards indicated—'

'Carlton Richards is an unbearable pompous ass, and if he indicated that I was in his corner, let me correct the notion. The fact is, I agreed to hear the thing Monday because the district attorney requested it. My understanding is that he plans to reduce the charge against Walters from a felony to a misdemeanour.'

'That's what Mr Richards told me.' Margie looked straight at the judge. 'But frankly, I'm not certain he has enough information to make that kind of decision.'

She could not tell if it was humour or disapproval that shone in the judge's eyes. 'I take it you don't agree that this act by Walters was only a childish prank.'

Nonplussed by his casual tone, Margie set her cup down. As long as he was willing to listen, she was going to make her point.

'For one thing, Judge Wendell, I've discovered that Glenn Walters has had a long-standing relationship with Anna Hardesty. He had been harassing her for several weeks before he mutilated her cat, which is consistent with a history of harassment and bizarre behaviour both here and in Arizona.'

'Is he dangerous?'

'Potentially, yes, Your Honour. He is entirely egocentric. He is motivated by self-gratification, and he exhibits no remorse. In my professional opinion, without intervention, he will continue to be a threat to society.'

'I see.' The judge rose to pour more tea. 'You've documented that in your report.'

'Insofar as possible, yes, and Judge Maitland in Juvenile Division has sub-poenaed juvenile records that I think will bear out my findings.'

A telephone buzzed in the vacant outer office, but the judge made no move to answer it. 'You've been very thorough,' he told Margie. 'And I do appreciate your concerns, but you realize that if the district attorney reduces the charges, I will likely be forced to release Walters with counselling as a condition of probation.'

Margie nodded, her attention distracted by the continued buzzing of the phone. She had no idea where the court clerk was, but she was glad when Judge Wendell pushed a button on his own phone and finally took the call.

Once again she was struck by the similarities between Glenn Walters and Roy Gates—cunning sociopaths with clever attorneys who could twist the facts to their advantage. She was prepared to point out, as she had in her report, that Walters would very likely flee, but she knew it didn't matter. The judge's decision would be bound by whatever charges the DA brought.

She was mulling that over when Judge Wendell leaned forward and handed the receiver to her. Surprised, she held the instrument to her ear. 'This is Margie Reed.'

She listened for a moment and thanked the caller, then hung up and looked at the judge.

'That was Chet Anderson,' she told him quietly. 'He thought I would want to know. Anna Hardesty, the victim in this case, died about an hour ago...'

It seemed to Trisha, as she gazed out the window, that she had spent too many hours of her married life staring out into the wind and rain, watching and waiting for her husband to get home safely.

She looked at Rob, who was napping peacefully, with Rebecca beside him, on Margie's queen-size bed. She knew she should feel better now, encouraged, even hopeful that their lives would become more peaceful. Still she could not seem to shake the sense of foreboding that had haunted her for days.

She jumped as a bolt of lightning split the darkened sky; then she turned back to the window to wait uneasily for the clap of thunder that would follow. She had read somewhere that Southern California got fewer than thirty days of rain per year. No wonder, she thought, if even a few of them were as monumental as this!

The rain pounded in heavy sheets on the brick walkway below and glistened ominously on the blacktopped street beyond the perimeter of the apartment complex. Without intending to, she focused her gaze on the corner across the street, where yesterday she would have sworn that someone was standing and watching her.

She tried to tell herself that her imagination had simply been working overtime. She was spooked because of the murder next door, edgy because of her problems.

Breathe deeply, she scolded herself. *Everything's under control.* But she jumped in spite of herself at the sudden, sharp, insistent ring of the phone.

'Hello,' she ventured, picking it up and carrying it out into the hall, feeling her body go slack with relief when she recognized Margie's voice.

'Hi, Trisha,' her sister-in-law said. 'Are

you all staying warm and dry?'

'Yes. Rob and the baby are sleeping. I was'—she hesitated—'just looking out the window.'

Margie paused. 'Are you all right? Your voice sounds kind of funny. Trisha, I hope you're not catching a cold—'

'No. No, I'm fine. Maybe a little jittery. Maybe the rain's got me down.'

Margie laughed. 'I was about to say that it never rains like this out here. But that's what people always say when the weather doesn't behave.'

Trisha tried to laugh along with her, but it came out sounding like a croak.

Margie paused again. 'Are you sure you're okay? Tell me, if something's wrong.'

Trisha wavered. She wanted to tell her that she had this awful feeling...but that was silly. She was perfectly fine, and Rob was right here with her...

'Nothing's wrong,' she said finally. 'Really. It must be the rain.'

'Well, if you're sure. Listen, Trisha, I won't be home for dinner. Paul is picking me up at the hospital. I'll see you a little later.'

Trisha bit her lip. She was glad for Margie. Glad she was seeing Paul. If she could just get rid of these silly jitters, everything would be just fine.

'Good,' she said, as heartily as she could. 'Have a super time. And don't worry. We're all okay. We'll see you whenever you get home...'

CHAPTER 25

It appeared to Sergeant Ray Nance that the worst of the storm was over. A light rain dribbled desultorily over the swollen earth, but the greyness had lifted and patches of blue pierced through the swiftly moving clouds.

Stretching to ease his tired neck muscles, he glanced down at his notes. It was four o'clock. Maybe he could reach Jennifer Hernandez, the social worker in Mendocino.

He dialled the number of the storefront health clinic in a remote part of the county. 'Sergeant Ray Nance in Santa Barbara again,' he said. 'Has Ms Hernandez returned?'

The phone rang seven times before it was answered and the social worker was brusque. She was interrupted several times in the course of listening to his spiel.

'Kiefer,' he told her. 'Dennis Kiefer. He's a transient, has been for some time.

According to information provided by the Mendocino County Sheriff, you saw him at the clinic on August second of last year. I was hoping you could tell me something about him, his background, why he came in...'

'You've got to be kidding,' Hernandez said. 'August of last year. Do you have any idea how many people pass through here, how many I see in a week?'

Nance grimaced. 'Yes, Ms Hernandez. You're overworked and underpaid. So am I, but I'm looking for a killer and I need to know more about him. You must have records. Could you dig them out? I'll be happy to hold the line.'

The social worker sighed heavily. 'Hang on. I'll see what I can find.'

While he waited, he reviewed the notes he'd taken earlier in the day, wrested with difficulty from three other social workers in different parts of the state.

Kiefer was reported as being personable and cooperative, reasonable and realistic, deferential and appreciative. He was a model client, Nance reflected wryly, except for a minor aberration: a penchant for killing people when they got in his way or when they had something he wanted.

'Are you still there?' Hernandez was back.

'Yes. Did you find your file?'

'Yes, hang on, I'm flipping through... trying to read my own notes... Here it is. Walk-in. Dennis Kiefer. Twelve thirty p.m. Transient, says he'll work for food and a place to sleep and shower.'

'Was he sick?'

'I don't think so, since I didn't note it. Just that he wanted help. Seems sincere, pleasant manner...that's what I wrote in my notes.'

Nance ran a hand across the back of his neck. 'Did he give you any history?'

'Let's see...he said he'd been on his own since he was eleven years old. He ran away from his father's home in Seattle, Washington, after his mother deserted. Said he'd worked on the docks, worked in lumber mills...couldn't find work in California.'

I'll bet, Nance thought. 'What'd you do for him?'

'Referred him to a neighbourhood shelter. It's run by a local council of churches. They'd provide him with a bed for a couple of nights, feed him, and send him on his way.'

And two days later, he'd kill a young woman by the name of Amy Howard and check into Mendocino County Hospital, where nobody would think to look.

Nance shook his head. Enough, already. The pattern was pretty evident. He thanked

Hernandez, hung up the phone, and picked up the receiver again.

It had been Seller's idea to check unsolved crimes against Kiefer's hospital gigs. Now it was time to tell him what he'd learned. He dialled the lieutenant in Santa Clarita.

It was just after five when Mack buzzed Margie to let her know Paul was there.

'Send him back here,' she said, closing a file folder and beginning to tidy up her desk.

He appeared in her doorway wearing a boyish grin and a yellow rain slicker over his clothing. He held out another slicker. 'For you,' he said. 'It's not glamorous, but it keeps you dry. If you're like the rest of us, you didn't take a raincoat when you left home this morning either.'

Margie smiled, touched by his thoughtfulness and surprised at how glad she was to see him. 'You're right,' she said. 'I already got soaked once, on the way over to court.'

She got up, held out her arms and let him slip the slicker over her suit, laughing as he rolled up the too-long sleeves and fastened the metal grommets.

'I feel like a kid in kindergarten,' she said. 'Wearing my brother's hand-me-downs.'

'Sheriff's issue, and don't knock it, or I'll make you wear the hat.'

He pulled a stiff-brimmed, yellow plastic hat out of the pocket of his slicker, but Margie showed him her bedraggled umbrella. 'It's damp, but it'll do the trick.'

'What do you think?' he asked Mack, as he led her down the hall.

The guard grinned. 'I've seen ripe bananas with more pizzazz than that. But what the heck, it'll keep you dry if this rainstorm don't let up.'

He buzzed them out and they rode the elevator down to the main floor. 'You wait here,' Paul told Margie. 'I'll bring the car around.'

He took her to a restaurant just off the freeway that looked like an English pub. 'It's not fancy, but the food is good,' he told her, as they huddled under Margie's umbrella. 'Great fish and chips with malt vinegar. Perfect for a night like this.'

Inside, there was sawdust on the floor and the glow of hurricane lamps, and roughhewn wooden tables were grouped cozily around a great big potbellied stove. A cheerful waitress brought them mugs of beer and put a bowl of peanuts on the table. 'Six lashes,' she said, winking, 'for anyone too tidy to toss the empty shells on the floor.'

Margie felt her body relax in the warmth from the nearby stove. 'You're a natural caretaker.' She smiled at Paul. 'You always know the right thing to do.'

He shook his head sadly. 'I wish I did. Some things are tougher than others. Right now, I want to find this Kiefer...' He did not finish the sentence.

Margie looked at him. 'You're sure it's Kiefer.'

'The more I know, the surer I am. I'd stake anything on the fact that he killed Jeanne Kerns and Emma Danziger, too. He's a killer, Margie, a predatory animal. I want him off the streets.'

Margie knew he was concerned for her safety, though he did not elaborate on that. 'Do you know a little more about Kiefer now than you did the other night?'

Paul nodded. 'I'm getting a sort of a composite picture—a lot like the composite sketch. I just talked to a cop up in Santa Barbara who's hearing the same things I am.'

'Such as,' Margie prompted.

'The guy's a drifter. Been on his own since he was a kid. He's a chameleon, Margie, a real manipulator. That's how he manages to protect himself. He knows how to use the system and he blends into the environment. And he kills easily, too easily, whenever it suits his purpose.'

Paul was describing the classic sociopath, the human being without a conscience, but she saw immediately the distinct difference between this Kiefer and, say, Glenn Walters.

'Why did he kill Jeanne Kerns?' she asked.

'Because she had something he wanted. She took him home with her, he saw his chance, he killed her, and he robbed her.'

Margie nodded. 'And Emma Danziger?'

'I think she interrupted a robbery. He had broken into the nurses' locker room. Danziger found him in a nearby office and he killed her.'

'In other words, he's an impulsive killer.'

'Yes. I guess you could say that.'

'And this is the man—be honest, Paul—the man you think is stalking me.'

She kept quiet as the waitress approached and took their order for fish and chips. Then she looked up. 'Why?' she asked. '*Why* do you think he's stalking me.'

'Because, Margie, whether your subconscious mind will allow you to recall it or not, you saw him in the stairwell the night he killed Kerns and he knows it. He saw you, too. That's why I showed you that sketch this afternoon. I was hoping it would ring a bell.'

Margie shook her head. 'I didn't see anyone. I do think that someone saw me.

But if it was Kiefer, why has he waited? Why hasn't he killed me yet?'

'There's only one reason I can think of, Margie. He hasn't had the opportunity.'

'The opportunity? Paul, really—'

'Think about it, Margie. Please. You work in the hospital, in a prison ward, safe behind closed doors. You live minutes away, and ever since the night of that first murder, you've had a houseful of people living with you. Kiefer may be impulsive, but he's not stupid. He simply hasn't been able to get to you, which is why I want to find him, fast, before he sees his chance.'

The waitress brought their sizzling platters. 'Enjoy!' she told them brightly.

Margie looked at the food without appetite. Something was very wrong.

'Anna Hardesty died today,' she said, still looking at her plate.

'Who?'

'Anna Hardesty. The owner of the cat that Glenn Walters mutilated. He *could* have killed her. He could have killed Mrs Hardesty. Glenn told me that himself. But he didn't. He killed her cat instead, and left it for her to find...'

Paul picked up his fork. 'What are you saying?'

'I guess, that there are two types of sociopaths. The disorganized, like Kiefer, who kill on impulse. And the narcissistic, like Walters—who enjoy the game, who plan, who kill for revenge. They're the type who leave warnings...like the warnings Glenn left for Anna Hardesty...and the warnings someone's been leaving me...'

Paul looked at her. 'But you said yourself, those so-called messages could have been nothing but pure coincidence. A misdelivered funeral wreath, even a slashed tyre, don't necessarily qualify as *warnings!*'

Margie pushed food around on her plate. 'What about that list of former patients I gave you? You said you'd check it out.'

'I did, Margie. I'm still checking. There are a few I can't account for, but—'

She looked at him.

'I'm still checking. It's like looking—'

'For a needle in a haystack.'

Paul nodded. 'I'll do my best.'

'I know you believe it's Kiefer. But Kiefer doesn't fit the pattern of a cunning, organized killer. If these *are* warnings that someone's been leaving me, then you're not looking hard enough at the type of personality who would leave them.'

Paul placed a hand over hers. 'And maybe you're looking too hard. You're the psychologist but I'm the cop. We're playing on my turf now.'

In spite of everything, the fish tasted

good. Margie was hungrier than she had realized. She decided to try to salvage what was left of the evening and to think about all this later, on her own.

'I like this place,' she said lightly. 'You were right. The food is wonderful. A perfect place to come in out of the rain—yellow slicker and all.'

He was watching Margie as though he wanted to be sure that she had not closed herself off from him. Then he splashed vinegar over his fish and chips. 'Good,' he said. 'I'm glad.'

Troubled, but unwilling to think about why, Margie ate her dinner and allowed herself to be lulled by the food and the pine-scented warmth of the stove. They lingered over coffee, but at a little past nine Paul called for the check.

'I promised to get you home early,' he said. 'And that's what I'm going to do. Would I be pushing my luck if I asked about tomorrow night?'

Margie shook her head. 'Tomorrow's Friday. I can't,' she said. 'There's a meeting I have to go to at the hospital.'

And, she remembered, *I'll be taking Rob for his first appointment with Chet...*

Outside, water dripped from the eaves and chill canyon winds bent the row of young elms that lined the restaurant parking lot. But the rain had stopped,

261

leaving deep puddles that reflected watery images.

'It hasn't stormed like this in October for as far back as I can remember,' Paul told her, rubbing his hands to warm them as he slipped into the driver's seat.

Margie smiled. 'Why do people always say things like that? In Connecticut, we used to tell the vacationers that every snowstorm they happened to get caught in was the worst we'd ever seen.'

'Do you miss the snow?'

'Not yet,' she said. 'But I'll probably miss the skiing.'

'Maybe not. I'll take you to Big Bear. Maybe even Mammoth. Either one's only a few hours drive, and the skiing's pretty good, even when folks down here in the flatlands are basking in eighty-degree weather.'

Margie closed her eyes, suddenly confronted with a barrage of conflicting feelings, mostly having to do with disloyalty to Frank and attraction to the man who sat beside her.

She said nothing as Paul drove in silence back to Santa Clarita Hospital. He turned into the vast parking area and around toward the back of the building.

It had begun to rain again, large, fat drops spattering heavily against the windshield. Paul turned the wipers on, but the road ahead was blurred.

Margie saw it first, and her sharp intake of breath made Paul hit the brakes hard, nearly sending them into a spin and jolting them both forward.

Emblazoned on the trunk of Margie's Honda was a ragged, red *X*, its lower extensions blurring in the rain and beginning to drip over the back bumper like rivulets of bright red blood.

CHAPTER 26

There was a new case folder on her desk Friday morning, a request for evaluation of a convicted arsonist with a record in three states. Margie tried to read the court order, but her concentration was splintered and she found herself reading the same paragraph two and three times over.

She looked out the window into the grey morning, dark with the threat of more rain, and wondered if the police photographer had already been there to photograph the back of her car.

Paul had taken on a calm authority when he saw the painted *X* last night, his voice deadly quiet and his jaw set as he insisted on driving her home.

'I'll pick you up in the morning, too,' he'd told her. 'You are not to move that vehicle till I okay it.'

Margie was intensely glad that she was not given to panic. She'd managed to recover from her initial shock and accept his terse directive and resist the urge to put into words what was now clear to both of them: There was nothing random or coincidental about this latest, graphic message. Margie was the target of a demented plan to scare the wits out of her—or worse.

Closing the folder, she thought again about her conversation with Paul last night and her growing realization that their professional judgments were widely and alarmingly divergent.

Paul was searching for a transient killer with a history of haphazard behaviour; he was convinced that the man's motive for terrorizing Margie was fear that she could identify him. But the more Margie learned about Dennis Kiefer, the more certain she was that Paul was wrong.

Whoever was tormenting her was cunning and calculating, intelligent and able to plan. Like Glenn Walters, he seemed to fit the prototype of the *organized* offender. It didn't seem likely that this Dennis Kiefer would exhibit those kind of traits.

Margie got up and paced the small

office. She was filled with a restless energy and wondered suddenly whether her professional judgement was clouded by her personal fears. Paul *was,* after all, a cop, a homicide investigator with years of experience tracking all kinds of criminals. Could she really believe that his fear for her safety was somehow clouding *his* judgment?

She closed her eyes, as if something so simple could keep her from facing something else: the gnawing awareness that she cared for Paul deeply and that he cared for her. She knew, as surely as she knew anything, that the relationship was coming to a crossroad. Soon—very soon—there would be no denying their physical or emotional attraction.

What she didn't know was whether she was ready to let go of the past or to make any kind of commitment at all when the future seemed so uncertain.

'Penny for your thoughts?'

She opened her eyes. Chet was standing in the doorway, concern etched in the boyish face she had come to know and trust.

'I was just thinking,' she said sadly. 'I'm a sorry excuse for a psychologist. Here I am, chastising my brother for locking himself into the past, coercing him to talk to a total stranger, forcing him to face the truth, and I can't seem to face it myself. I can't seem to separate what I feel in my heart from what's going on in my head...'

Chet shrugged. 'Occupational hazard. Physician, heal thyself. Listen, Margie, you're a damned good psychologist, but you can't be your own patient.'

She smiled despite herself. 'I know that.'

'I know you do. Quit trying, and let life happen.'

Let life happen. She linked an arm through his. 'Come on. I owe you a cup of coffee.'

'You're on.'

'Where's my cheese Danish?'

'You hate cheese Danishes.'

'That's beside the point. You owe me one. How's Phyllis?' she asked in the hallway.

'Bearing up, I think. She thought she was prepared for the fact that her mother might die, but of course nobody ever really is.'

'No,' Margie agreed. 'Nobody ever is. You'll be good for her, Chet, I know you will.'

He followed Margie into the elevator. 'I hope so. She's good for me. I'll be seeing her again later tonight, whenever I can get away.'

'Oh, Chet! You'll be seeing Rob! Listen,

266

if you'd rather put it off...'

He shook his head. 'No,' he told her. 'It wasn't easy to convince him to see me. I told Phyllis I'd be at her place by ten. There's no reason to cancel.'

She was prepared to argue, but Chet was adamant, and in a way Margie was relieved. It seemed to her that Rob had been a little edgy the past few days. She thought he might be nervous about seeing Chet. It would be best to keep this appointment tonight and get him started in therapy.

'Hey, leadfoot, are you okay or would you rather I do the driving?'

Paul instinctively eased up on the accelerator and looked over at Ellen. 'Sorry,' he muttered. 'No, I'm fine. Just in a hurry, I guess.'

The purple haze had lifted from the mountains and the sky was a hopeful blue-grey, but the weatherman promised more rain was on the way, and Paul figured the inclement weather might force Kiefer off the streets.

With Ellen's help, he'd covered the hospitals within a fifty-mile radius of Santa Clarita, but there were several shelters for the homeless in the area, and he was determined to alert them all. If that lunatic turned up in any one of them, he wanted to know about it pronto.

He heard his call number on the car's radio. 'This is Sellers. What's up?'

The dispatcher's voice was mushy with static. 'The '87 Honda's been cleared. Leon checked it out stem to stern. He said you wanted to know.'

Paul nodded. It hadn't seemed likely that the car, once marked, would have been tampered with. But he'd wanted it checked out just to be on the safe side, before Margie got behind the wheel.

'What about the damage to the paint?' he asked.

'Leon cleaned it up. Nothing permanent.'

Paul nodded, signed off, and turned his attention to his driving.

The crudely painted X had already begun to run by the time they saw it in the rain last night, which didn't say much for the intelligence quotient of the son of a bitch who painted it. Paul had covered the car with a canvas tarp to preserve the damage until the photographer could shoot it. He was glad to know a new paint job wasn't necessary before Margie saw the car again.

She'd been great last night, level-headed in spite of her shock, and she'd had the good grace not to point out to Paul that the incident was clearly not *coincidence*.

Paul, like Margie, recognized the urgency in this latest graphic message. He did not want to think about what might happen if he didn't find Kiefer soon.

He must have been pressing down harder on the gas, because Ellen was looking at him sideways. 'Okay,' he said. 'I get the message. What's the number on Oak?'

The Valley Shelter was a rundown building just north of the railroad tracks, a converted warehouse with peeling green paint and a grubby window storefront. Paul parked in the alley, next to a grey-bearded wino who was either passed out or dead, and without bothering to find out which, he headed straight for the storefront.

'Chee-wowa,' Ellen muttered as the stench assaulted their nostrils, an acrid mix of urine, stale sweat, and something like cabbage soup.

The square front room, sparsely fur-nished with wooden picnic tables and battered metal folding chairs, held ten or twelve men and a couple of women in various outlandish getups, some playing cards, others talking, and three or four sound asleep. Paul did not need to tell them that he was a cop. They'd made him for one the minute they saw him, and their voices hushed as he looked around from one wary face to another. When he was sure he had their attention, he spoke in a low voice.

'I'm looking for a guy named Kiefer,' he said. He let the name hang in the air. 'Dennis Kiefer, early twenties, a drifter, been up and down the state. He's a mean one, just as soon kill you as not, and I want him real bad, real fast. I brought some pictures you can all take a look at. I can make it worth your while to remember him.'

Their faces were blank, but Ellen began to pass around copies of Kiefer's likeness. Paul walked past them to what his nose told him was a kitchen in the rear of the building.

A burly guy with the florid face of a one-time alcoholic looked up briefly from the pot he was stirring and then turned to his task.

'Sheriff's Lieutenant Sellers,' Paul began. 'You the guy that runs this place?'

'Christian Charities runs it,' the man mumbled. 'I work here for room and board. Two other guys come in to help at night. Most nights, anyways.'

'What's your name?'

'Clarence Halloran.'

'How many do you sleep here, Halloran?'

The man shrugged. 'Eighteen, twenty, I guess. When the weather's bad, like it has been, we pack 'em in wall to wall.'

Paul showed him the sketch of Kiefer. 'Ever see this guy?'

Halloran studied it. 'Nope. Not here. Not that I recall.'

'Anywhere.'

'No. I never seen him.'

Paul nodded slowly. Then he reached into his coat pocket, drew out a business card and took it with the sketch, to a greasy bulletin board on one wall of the kitchen.

'Listen, Halloran.' He found a tack and posted the sketch and the card. 'When your buddies come in, I want 'em to see this. It could mean somebody's life. If you see this guy, I want to know. Immediately. I'll make it worth your while.'

Halloran picked up a rusting cleaver and began to chop some carrots. 'You got it.'

'Good. Thank you, Halloran. I was hoping you'd understand.'

Ellen was already out of the building, standing near the car, poking gingerly at the wino's ribs with the toe of one low-heeled pump.

The man moaned, turned on his side, and began snoring loudly. Ellen cast an irreverent look skyward and got into the car.

There were six babies in plastic contraptions on the other side of the glass—four boys and two girls, if he could trust the colours of the blankets. Five were sleeping, but one of the boys was screaming to beat the band. Denny watched the way his cheeks puffed up and his tiny face reddened.

You, kid, he said to himself, *will grow up to be king of the hill. You'll run rings and circles around these other nerds. You watch. You'll get anything you want.*

He watched for a minute, then stepped back from the glass and started up the hall, figuring it was time to get out of the nursery before someone noticed him standing there.

'You!'

Resisting the urge to run, Denny turned around slowly.

A stern-faced nurse eyed him suspiciously. He gave her his nicest smile.

'Are you an orderly?'

'Yes, ma'am,' he said.

'Good. Follow me.' She went to the desk and picked up some folders. 'These need to go down to the business office. Do you know where it is?'

Denny nodded.

'First floor. Behind the admitting desk.'

'Yes, ma'am.' He smiled again. 'I'll take them right on down.'

Taking the folders, he turned on his heel and headed back up the hall, pleased that he'd thought to take off his name tag before he went into the nursery.

He considered dumping the stack of folders into the nearest trash can, but then he figured someone might look for him if they didn't get delivered. He waited for the elevator, stepped inside, and pushed the first-floor button.

He dropped the folders on a counter in the business office and was on his way out when he saw it. For a minute he froze. He looked at the drawing. It was *his* face!

His heart beating faster, he glanced from the drawing to the street outside the main entrance. Rain was coming down in buckets again. What the hell should he do?

'Was there something else you wanted?'

A skinny blonde woman was getting up from her desk. She was looking at him! Coming toward him! He wanted to run, but he didn't dare. He began to walk slowly.

Easy, he told himself, *nice and easy. A few more steps to the elevator. In with the crowd. Off on nine. Stairs the rest of the way.*

He slipped into the stairwell and took the three flights, his heart beating wildly. He did not rest until he'd reached the twelfth floor and shut the heavy metal door behind him.

CHAPTER 27

'I saw some cards and games in the hall closet. Would you like to play some canasta?'

Rob did not look up from his magazine.

'Checkers?' Trisha asked.

'Dammit, Trisha, only you would think of games at a time like this!'

'It's raining outside. That's what people do. They play games on a rainy day.'

Rob threw the magazine across the room. 'Well, it isn't what I do, okay?'

Trisha felt tears sting the back of her eyelids. 'What *do* you do, Rob? Tell me. You've been grouching around here like a caged animal. Can't you tell me what's bothering you?'

He did not answer, but she could tell by looking at him that he was stretched tighter than a rubber band. She knew what it was: the appointment was tonight. He was going to see a psychiatrist, and he was going to have to talk about whatever it was that had been driving him crazy for months.

Trisha watched him. He was nervous, that was all. She ought to be able to understand that. She could try harder.

She could let him know how glad she was that he was going.

'Rob,' she said, 'it's the shrink, isn't it? You're nervous about talking to Margie's friend. But you'll see, Rob, it's going to be fine, the best thing you ever did—'

'Dammit, Trish, I'm going, aren't I? I don't want to talk about it, too. Get the cards and play some solitaire, and for Pete's sake, leave me alone!'

Tears sprang to her eyes again, but she didn't want Rob to see them. She got up and checked on Rebecca, who was sleeping soundly on Margie's bed. She got a deck of cards from the hall closet and brought them back to the living room.

On the way she stopped at the window and looked out into the rain, half expecting—she didn't know what. Someone staring up at her again?

That was part of it, she told herself firmly, sitting down to shuffle the cards. She'd been jittery herself these past few days. Her imagination was working overtime. No wonder she wasn't able to cope with Rob—she could barely cope with herself.

She moved some magazines off the oak coffee table and dealt out a hand of solitaire. Queen on the king. Nine on the ten. An ace up in the corner.

'Trisha?'

'Yes?'

'I'm sorry, hon. I shouldn't take it out on you. You're right. I'm nervous. I don't want to go. If only I hadn't promised Margie...'

Seven on the eight. Jack on the queen. 'You aren't going for Margie.'

'I know. I know. I'm going for myself. And you, Trish. I'm going for you. You and Rebecca, because I love you both. I want you to know that. I love you.'

She wanted to believe him. She *did* believe him, but she didn't trust herself to speak. She turned three cards. Ten on the jack. Deuce of clubs on the ace. She concentrated on the turn of the cards and the sound of the rain outside.

'I won,' she said.

'What?'

'I won! Look, I turned all the cards.'

'Good for you.'

'I hardly ever do that. I'll take it as a lucky sign.' She gathered up the cards and looked at her watch. 'Margie ought to be home soon. Would you like something to eat before you go? Margie ought to eat something, too.'

She went to the kitchen and opened the cupboard. It was a good night for soup. 'Rob, would you like some soup?' she called.

'Fine. Soup is fine.'

276

'What kind?'

'I don't care.'

'There's vegetable beef, tomato, or chicken and rice.'

'I don't care, I already told you, Trisha. Whatever you want is fine.'

She walked to the living room. '*You* choose. We'll have whichever you want.'

'Dammit, Trisha, what's the matter with you? Can't you make a simple decision?'

Rebecca started crying. Trisha was stunned. She struggled to find her voice. 'Yes, Rob, I can. I travelled three thousand miles with a little baby, *because* I made a decision.'

'Yes, you did!' Rob stood up, his voice rising angrily. 'And maybe I should have just let you go! You don't understand. You can't! It's *my* problem and *I* have to deal with it. I shouldn't have bothered to follow you!'

This time, the tears spilled over, hot and wet on her cheeks. Now Rebecca was screaming. She had to go get her. Trisha turned and ran from the room.

Judge Nathan Wendell removed his reading glasses, leaned back in his chair and gently massaged the bridge of his nose with his forefingers. It had begun to rain again and, he reminded himself, he was to be the keynote speaker at a reelection campaign dinner in Westwood in less than two and a half hours.

Ordinarily he paid little attention to the day-to-day plea bargains agreed to between prosecutors and defence attorneys. It was a fact of life that any number of defendants charged with major offences would ultimately answer to lesser charges. But it disturbed him still, after twenty years on the bench, when the reasons for such plea bargains seemed somehow contrived, as in the case of Glenn Walters.

It was not that he questioned the district attorney's ethics. Calvin Drury was both competent and responsible. However, it seemed to Judge Wendell that in the case of Glenn Walters, his decision was precipitous, based on information that was at worst faulty and at best less than complete.

Mason Eldridge, in a report commissioned by the defence, characterized Walters as immature and contrite, a young man whose poor self-image and lack of direction had brought him to adulthood with a skewed sense of judgment.

It was a far cry from Margie Reed's assessment, which was by far the more thorough. Her report concluded from the defendant's family history, and his previous acts of terrorism, his relationship with Anna Hardesty, and his stated lack of remorse that Walters displayed marked sociopathic tendencies that were likely to escalate without psychiatric intervention.

It was a moot point, Wendell realized, whether or not intervention would mitigate those sociopathic tendencies. But the opportunity for therapy would be lost altogether if Walters were released on probation and fled.

The judge put his glasses back on and read through the last of his notes. He wondered whether the district attorney was yet aware that Mrs Hardesty had died as a result of Walters's act. While it was, of course, the DA's decision to make, it seemed to Wendell that, all things considered, there was more of a case for charging Walters with involuntary manslaughter than for reducing the present charge to a misdemeanour.

Calvin Drury was a reasonable man. Judge Wendell consulted his watch and decided he had just enough time to call him.

Margie sensed there was something amiss the moment she entered her apartment.

Rob, who generally greeted her with a kiss, never looked up from the magazine he was reading as she stood in the doorway, shaking the water off her umbrella and standing it just outside the door.

'Hi!' she said, slipping out of her raincoat. 'It's wet out there, in case you hadn't noticed.'

'Mmm,' said Rob, his eyes on the magazine. 'Good night to stay indoors.'

Margie looked at him. 'Is something the matter?'

'I don't know. You're the shrink, remember?'

She frowned. 'Where are your girls?' she asked.

Rob shrugged. 'The bedroom, I guess.'

She hung her raincoat over the back of a chair and walked down the hall to the bedroom. 'There you are!' she called brightly. 'How are my favourite ladies?'

Rebecca, who was having her diaper changed, wiggled around and grinned. Trisha looked up. 'Hi,' she said, with less than her usual enthusiasm.

Margie sat on the bed with Rebecca, tickling her rounded tummy. The baby giggled, but Trisha scolded her, urging her to hold still.

Concerned in earnest, Margie drew her hand away and bent closer to the baby. 'Something's going on around here, Rebecca. Can you tell me what it is?'

She waited a moment, but Trisha said nothing. 'Trisha? How about you?'

Trisha reached for a sleeper suit and began to put it on the baby. 'Nothing,' she said. 'We had an argument. It really doesn't concern you.'

Margie debated the proper response. She decided there really wasn't one.

'I'm sorry,' her sister-in-law blurted suddenly, sitting on the bed. 'That was rude. Of course it concerns you. We're in your house, after all—'

'Please, Trisha. That has nothing to do with it. Your private life is your own. I'm sorry you argued, but if there's nothing I can do...' Her voice trailed away.

Tears welled in Trisha's eyes, but she wiped them away roughly. 'Maybe you should cancel this appointment tonight. I think that's what's bothering Rob. I don't think he wants to go through with it. He hasn't said so, but I know.'

Margie spoke quietly. 'If that's what Rob wants, of course I'll cancel the appointment. Therapy doesn't stand a chance if the patient isn't willing to cooperate.'

Trisha stroked her daughter's cheek. 'But that puts us right back where we started from.'

'Only if you're right. And I wouldn't dream of asking him if he wants to cancel. It will have to come from Rob. Maybe he *wants* to start, but he's feeling a little scared.'

Trisha nodded. 'There's something else.' She sighed. 'I really feel silly saying this—'

'Don't feel silly. Tell me what it is.'

Trisha turned away. 'I know this sounds dumb. I don't want to be alone. I've been sort of jumpy lately. I'm afraid to stay alone with the baby.'

Margie wondered if her own anxiety had somehow rubbed off on her sister-in-law. Not that it mattered. If Trisha was jumpy, she shouldn't be left alone.

'You know,' she said. 'I think I may know somebody who would love to have your company. Excuse me just a minute while I make a phone call.' She got up and left the room.

She called Chet from the kitchen phone. He thought it was a wonderful idea.

'Let me call Phyllis,' he told Margie. 'I'll call you back in a minute.'

Trisha and the baby were coming into the living room by the time Margie took the call. 'Trisha,' she said. 'You're so good with people. There's a woman whose mother just passed away. She says she'd be grateful if you and Rebecca could spend some time with her tonight.'

Rob looked up, obviously puzzled. She could see Trisha wavering.

'Her name is Phyllis Hardesty,' Margie told her. 'She's not much older than you are. She's a friend of Chet's, the psychologist I work with who'll be seeing Rob tonight.'

It was an opening for Rob, but he said nothing. Trisha put the baby in his lap.

'Wrap her in a blanket,' she said to her husband. 'I'll just get a jacket and some diapers.'

Margie looked at Rob. 'It's just a short drive. Do you want to come along for the ride? Or would you rather wait here, and I'll come back and change before we leave for the hospital?'

It was another opening, but Rob did not take it.

'I guess I'll ride along,' he said.

Trisha popped back into the living room. 'Rob? Have you seen the baby's Raggedy?'

He shrugged. 'No.'

'Well, that's funny. I could have sworn I saw it a while ago.'

Margie checked her watch. 'We have to get moving.'

'I know, but she loves it so.'

Rob stood up. 'For Pete's sake, Trisha! It's around. We'll find it later.'

Trisha blinked quickly. 'Okay, you're right. It's late. We'll look for it later.'

Denny paced his twelfth-floor sanctuary, moaning, muttering to himself...

That was crazy, coming back up here... where did they get that picture?...trapped, now

I'm trapped...I got things to do, important things to do...plus I'm starving. Haven't eaten since morning. What in hell should I do?

He looked out a window and listened to the rain. *Soon, it'll let up soon. Visiting hours, place'll be crowded. Got to take a chance, make a run for it.* He pulled the Piaget watch from his pocket. *Soon...pretty soon. Take a chance...*

CHAPTER 28

The phone was ringing when they came back in, Rob shielding Margie with the umbrella.

'Hello,' she said, running to answer it.

'Ms Reed? This is Calvin Drury.'

Margie paused. Drury was the district attorney. 'Yes, sir. What can I do for you?'

'I just had a phone call from Judge Wendell, Ms Reed. It's about your report on Glenn Walters.'

'Yes, sir. I left a copy with Judge Wendell and I left a copy in your office.'

'I thought you might have. I'm at home, Ms Reed. With a house full of dinner guests, I'm afraid. However, I would like to see it. Can you fax me a copy? I can

284

give you a number here.'

Margie had a copy in her briefcase, in the car. There was a fax machine at the hospital.

'I'm on my way back to the hospital,' she told him. 'I can fax you a copy from there.'

She wrote down the number, put it in her purse, and slipped out of her raincoat.

'Would you like some soup or something before we go?' Rob called from the kitchen.

Margie felt more rushed than hungry. 'No, thanks. I'll get something later. You go ahead. You must be hungry. I'll be ready in fifteen minutes.'

In the bedroom she stripped to her underwear. She felt chilled and damp clear through. A hot shower would be wonderful. She could fit one in if she hurried.

She went to her closet and rummaged through it, pulling out a blue wool dress. It was left over from her days in Connecticut, but tonight it was cool enough to wear it.

She wrapped a towel around her hair, thinking about the DA's request. Judge Wendell must have felt she had made some valid points if he'd bothered to call Calvin Drury. She wondered if Drury were as easy to persuade as Carlton Richards had implied.

In the bathroom she removed her makeup and looked at her reflection in the mirror. Was she mistaken, or did her skin look better than it had just a few weeks ago? It did, it seemed rosier, healthier somehow. It must be the dampness in the air.

Chiding herself for taking too much time, she reached for a big, fluffy towel. She laid it on the hamper, took off her bra and panties, and yanked the shower door open.

She was about to turn on the hot water when she saw it on the pink tile floor—Rebecca's Raggedy, slumped in the corner, its head resting on its lap.

How odd, Margie thought, reaching for the doll. *How did it get in the shower?* She picked it up, brought it toward her, and heard herself gasp for breath.

The doll's button eyes had been gouged out, and the little cloth face had been slashed—over and over, so that tufts of stuffing stuck out between the wounds. The mouth that had been a benign little smile drooped and hung grotesquely.

Margie stared at it, her pulse pounding. Then she began to shiver. She dropped the ruined doll to the floor and leaned for support against the sink.

Jumbled thoughts careened through her head. She struggled to sort through them. Another warning? Her blood ran cold. If it was, he was close. Too close. If it was, he was telling her, 'I have been in your house. I can get at you anytime...'

Shivering, she wrapped the towel around herself and crossed her arms in front of her, as if the act of hugging herself would somehow help to steady her. After a time she felt her heartbeat slow and felt the shuddering stop.

How? she asked herself. *How could someone have gotten into her house? They'd been gone, all of them, less than thirty minutes. Had he been watching? Waiting?*

She shook her head. It didn't seem possible. She was wrong, jumping to conclusions. She needed time to think it through, to find another explanation.

Rob! Was it Rob? Her blood ran cold again. Was her brother more troubled than she knew? Could he possibly be sick enough to do a thing like this? Why? To frighten her? Or Trisha?

He'd been angry with Trisha. He was angry with himself. But why take it out on the doll?

Then it struck her that Raggedy Ann was the doll Paul Sellers had brought. Paul, who in Rob's anguished mind, could be seen as taking Frank's place. Was Rob lashing out at Margie for seeing Paul? Did he think she was betraying him—and Frank?

She heard Rob calling, and she jumped at the sound. 'Marg? What's taking you so long?'

She swallowed hard. 'Almost ready. Five minutes is all I need.'

She turned on the hot water tap in the shower and jumped in almost immediately, holding her breath until the spray warmed up and sluiced over her body, soothing her.

She wanted to stay until she felt warm clear through, till the blood ran warm in her veins. But Rob was waiting and, more than ever, she wanted him to keep this appointment.

She turned off the water and stepped onto the mat, taking up the towel, rubbing her limbs as hard as she could, feeling the heat on her skin.

Rob had sounded so normal, calling her. *Could* he possibly have done this? Surely he would realize she'd be scared half to death, finding the ravaged doll. But if that were his intent, he would be relishing the moment, daring her not to show her fear.

Hold it, she told herself. *You may be a psychologist, but you know better than this. You know enough to resist the urge to try to analyse everything, especially when your personal involvement kicks objectivity out the window.*

Margie splashed cold water on her face to try to clear her head. She was going to have to deal with this somehow, regardless of who had destroyed the doll. For the moment, anyway, she was on her own. She would have to be alert and calm.

She scooped up the doll, wrapped it in a towel, and shoved it into the back of her closet. It would be easier for Trisha to accept that it was lost than to know what had actually happened to it. It was only a doll. It could be replaced. There was no point in dwelling on the symbolism.

Quickly she put on fresh underwear and pantyhose and slipped the blue dress over her head, then ran a brush through her short, dark hair and dabbed on lipstick and eye shadow.

'Coming!' she yelled when Rob knocked on the door. She stepped into a pair of black pumps. Bracing herself, she put a smile on her face and marched into the living room.

Rob, dressed in an all-weather coat over slacks and a tweed sport coat, was pacing near the front door, hands jammed into his pockets.

'Sorry,' she said, watching him closely as she put on her sodden raincoat. He was nervous, as he had been of late, but she could read nothing in his face.

There was a break in the rain and the

fall evening was a study in stark contrasts; patches of deepening turquoise sky in the last pink-gold slants of sunlight, a fluffy corona of amethyst clouds cresting the purple mountains.

'Would you like to drive?' she asked Rob, tossing him the keys.

He looked at the keys and tossed them back. 'No. No, I don't think so.'

'Tell me if it's none of my business,' she said, getting into the car. 'Trisha told me you'd argued today. She seemed a little upset.'

Rob made a clicking sound with his tongue. 'It doesn't take much to upset her these days. She's been as jumpy as a cat. But yes, whether it's your business or not, we did have an argument today.'

'Were you angry with her?' Margie ventured.

'Yes. I was at the time.'

Margie bit her lip. *Enough to punish her by slashing the Raggedy Ann? Was it Trisha who was supposed to have gotten into the shower before I even got home?*

'Look,' Rob said. 'I've told Trisha, whether she believes it or not, I love her. This has nothing to do with Trisha. It's something I have to work out myself.'

'You'll have help now,' Margie pointed out. 'It's a wonder you're not angry with me. After all, it's my fault, isn't it, that

290

you're going into therapy?'

Rob seemed to hesitate. 'I am a little sore at you. I still don't know if I want to go through with this. I feel as though you're pushing me into it.'

Margie was silent. There was nothing to say. She felt cold and scared and violated, and the image of the ravaged Raggedy Ann floated in and out of her consciousness.

It broke her heart to think that her brother might have committed such a savage act. But if he hadn't, then someone else had. She gripped the steering wheel harder.

CHAPTER 29

It was nearly dark when they reached the hospital and Margie drove into the parking lot. By the time she realized it was after hours and she could park anywhere she liked, she had circled the building out of force of habit and parked in her usual spot.

'Well,' she said, working hard to keep her voice even. 'Here we are. Santa Clarita Hospital. This is where I work.'

Rob nodded. 'A hospital's a hospital. They all look pretty much the same.

Better take your umbrella with you, in case it rains some more.'

She tucked the umbrella under her arm and started walking toward the entrance. 'The meeting I have to go to is in the main floor auditorium, but we'll go up to my floor first. That way, I can introduce you to Chet, so he doesn't seem like such a stranger.'

She watched Rob out of the corner of her eye. His expression told her nothing, but she suddenly felt as though they were kids again and she was dragging him to church against his will.

'Remember Mrs Fenstermacher?'

Margie turned to him, startled. It was almost as though he'd read her mind.

'Mrs Fenstermacher,' he said again. 'The youth leader at Good Shepherd's Church.'

'I remember, yes.' Margie managed a smile. 'She used to corner me every Tuesday night. She was always after me to bring you with me. She said you had a talent for evasion.'

Rob smiled wryly. 'I guess she was right. Like they say, some things never change...'

Margie was deliberating the significance of the remark as they entered the hospital lobby. She saw that a number of her hospital colleagues were filing into the

292

auditorium. She was going to be late. There was no way around it. She led the way to the elevators.

'Don't be put off by the security door,' she told Rob as they waited to be admitted. 'This is where our offices are, and it's the simplest place to meet.'

Chet met them halfway down the hall and Margie made the introductions, relieved that her brother seemed slightly more at ease than he had a little while earlier.

'I'm going to have to run,' she told him. 'I'm due at that meeting in the auditorium downstairs. I expect it will take a couple of hours. I'll meet you later in the main lobby and then we'll pick up Trisha and the baby.'

It was not until she'd made her way out again that she gave in to the trembling in her legs and leaned against the wall while she waited for the elevator, her mind moving in circles.

It occurred to her to skip the meeting altogether, to call Paul and tell him about the doll. If nothing else, he could make arrangements to have her building watched. But then, if it turned out Rob was the culprit, she would have wasted Paul's time and taken him away from his all-out search for the transient, Dennis Kiefer.

Kiefer, she thought, closing her eyes,

riding down in the elevator. Was Kiefer really at the root of all this? Was *he* the one she should be concerned with?

Again and again she turned it over in her mind. Kiefer. Rob. *Who?* She couldn't find the answer, no matter how she tried.

It didn't help that the auditorium doors were standing wide open when she reached them, and that the medical director, with whom she'd interviewed for her job, was standing off to one side.

'Good evening, Ms Reed.' He nodded curtly. 'I presume you are planning to join us.'

Sighing softly, she returned his greeting and entered the auditorium, slipping as unobtrusively as she could into a seat in the last row. She was going to have to report on this meeting to the others in her department. She was going to have to try to clear her mind and pay attention to what was said.

A tall, black woman was on the platform, a woman Margie recognized from the personnel services department. She was saying something about photo ID cards, something about increased security. Margie realized she had missed most of it. She would have to get it later, from someone else...

She began to wonder what was happening upstairs, how Chet was getting along with Rob. Would he even make a dent in the solid stone wall her brother had set up around himself? What kind of guilt was so heinous to Rob that he thought he must carry it alone?

The woman had finished speaking and was introducing someone else. Margie rummaged in her purse for a notebook and pen. She ought to take some notes.

'...to tell you more,' the woman said, 'about this new policy for interdepartmental communication, I will turn the programme over to the physician who proposed it: Dr Ira Jablonsky.'

Margie had finally found a pen and was putting her purse down beside her when she heard the name. She looked up sharply. Jablonsky. She knew the name.

He must be short, she said to herself. She was having trouble seeing him. She sat up tall and craned her neck to see around the people in front of her.

Finally she caught a glimpse of the speaker. Short. Paunchy. Balding. Margie frowned. That wasn't right. Jablonsky. Ira Jablonsky...

In an instant, it hit her—the surly young staffer she'd shared a table with in the cafeteria, the one who had shovelled in mountains of food while she nibbled away at her yogurt.

She looked away. Ira Jablonsky. That's

what his name tag had said. She tried to concentrate, picture the face. He'd been wearing a paper scrub net.

Then she realized something else, and she felt herself stop breathing. The sketch of Kiefer—the one Paul had shown her, right there in the cafeteria! Take away the paper hairnet and the face was one and the same.

Oh, God! she thought, glancing around her. *I have to get to Paul! He's combing the countryside for the missing transient, and Kiefer may have been here all along!*

'Excuse me,' she said, gathering up her purse, nearly forgetting her umbrella. She stood up and made her way past two startled nurses who'd come in after her.

Finally she was in the aisle, her legs like rubber under her, moving, walking out of the auditorium, over to the bank of telephones.

She threw the damp raincoat in a heap at her feet and the umbrella down on top of it. Change for the phone. In her purse, fingers fumbling. Where would Paul be? At the station?

Thank you, God. He is. He is 'Paul? Paul, it's Margie. I'm at the hospital, Santa Clarita. I think Kiefer may be here.'

She tried to explain what she'd found out about the man in the cafeteria. 'He was wearing a name tag, but it wasn't his.

296

He was only *posing* as a doctor. And the sketch! Paul, the drawing you showed me. That was *him!* The same face...'

When was it? Three days ago? Yes. Yes, it was Tuesday.

Paul spoke to her, quietly, soothing. 'Go back in to your meeting. Do you hear me, Margie? You'll be safest there. Go on back. I'm on my way.'

Hang up the phone. Relax. Breathe. Feeling back in my fingers. Better. Better. He's on his way. Back. Back to the meeting...

'I want every officer you can round up. Ten or a dozen if you can get them.'

Paul spoke with quiet authority, and the dispatcher moved to the radio.

'Code two,' he said. 'No lights, no sirens. Get 'em there on the double. Meet in the lobby for further instructions. And phone the hospital ahead. Let them know we're on our way, so nobody panics when we get there.'

He thought of Kiefer, holed up like a cockroach, somewhere at Santa Clarita. And Margie, under the same roof. He felt his jaw tighten.

'Rain's starting,' Ellen told him. 'Here. You'll want your slicker. Want me to drive?'

'Sure. Why not?' He was moving as he pulled on the slicker.

Margie tried to focus her attention on what was happening on the platform. She felt better, more in control, but her mind continued to wander.

Every sense, every nerve ending seemed to converge on Kiefer. Paul was right. She was wrong. It had to be Kiefer all along. Dressed as a doctor, he'd had free access, in and out of the hospital. The funeral wreath. The slashed tyre. The message on her car. The doll!

She slumped in her chair, weak with relief. How could she have thought it was Rob? Rob might be fighting his private demons, but he could never do a thing like that.

Her ears strained for a sound in the lobby, for a signal that Paul was there. But she heard nothing, not even much of what was being said on the platform. She thought again of the ravaged doll, in her shower, in her own house...

A sliver of doubt invaded her senses, but she fought to keep it away. She had never evaluated Dennis Kiefer. If she had, she might have realized, she might have known that despite his simplicity, despite his impulsive nature, he was capable of finding pleasure in leaving those ominous warnings.

The thought put her in mind of Glenn,

and she found herself squirming in her seat. Glenn, the omnipotent, the narcissistic stalker. A different kind of sociopath... No. She wouldn't think about that. She wasn't going to think about Glenn.

Then she suddenly sat straight up. Glenn! Her report on Glenn! She had promised to fax it to the district attorney, but in all the confusion she'd forgotten!

She looked around her. Should she leave again? Paul had told her to stay. But the district attorney would be waiting for the fax. He needed to see that report.

It was just after nine. Plenty of time before she had to meet Rob. All she had to do was run to the car, get her briefcase, and come back. The fax machine was in the business office, right off the main lobby. The police would be here any minute. And Paul. She would see Paul.

CHAPTER 30

At nine fifteen a dozen sheriff's deputies had assembled in the hospital lobby. Visiting hours were over, and by nine twenty-two Paul had posted sentries at every conceivable exit and dispersed the rest of them to fan out in teams through every floor of the building.

'Miss nothing,' he'd instructed them tersely. 'Every office, every stairwell, every boiler room *closet* is to be checked, rechecked, and checked again. If Kiefer is anywhere—*anywhere* in this building, I want him, and I want him fast.'

He turned to Ellen. 'The twelfth floor is ours. It's a natural nest for this insect—dark, deserted, and full of junk that's been stored there for the past two years. Investigators combed it the night the nurse was found, but that may have been before Kiefer found it.'

They rode the elevator up to eleven, then took the main stairwell, moving silently up the last flight of stairs to the hospital's uppermost floor. Paul sidled up to the door and peered through the pane of glass, his hand resting on the butt of his revolver, his ears alert to every sound.

It was dark inside, too dark to decipher anything more than shapes, the asymmetric, blocklike formations looming in every direction. Nodding to Ellen, he yanked the door open and listened for the sound of movement. Nothing. They waited for their eyes to adjust and moved into the darkened corridor.

In the eerie, hollow, empty silence, he heard the drip of water, and his gaze shifted to a porcelain sink in an alcove on the far right. His senses picked up nothing else, not a hint of human presence.

A sudden, brilliant bolt of lightning illuminated the corridor briefly, and he heard Ellen's muffled gasp at the crack of thunder that followed.

'Kiefer! Police!' His voice echoed in the dark, cavernous space. But he knew it was useless. Kiefer wasn't in there. Paul lowered his revolver and reached to pull out his flashlight.

Ellen followed suit, the two of them moving around stacks of crates and furnishings. It was she who found the first evidence that someone else had been there.

'Look,' she whispered, directing a beam of light at the space between two mattresses. Wedged between them was a Hershey bar wrapper, crumpled but unmistakable.

He moved the top mattress aside with his foot and the two of them looked at each other, then back at the cache of empty candy wrappers that littered the mattress underneath.

Ellen had kicked apart two other mattresses and was bending to examine some jewellery when Paul heard the crackle of static from the radio hooked to his belt.

'Fernandez on ten,' the voice sputtered.

'I think we've got him cornered. I spotted him crouched in the stairwell here, right outside the cafeteria. But he made us about the same time, and he took off down the stairs.'

'Who's pursuing?'

'We've got guys all over. What do you want to do with him when we get him?'

'Cuff him and hold him,' Sellers said. 'And let me know the minute you do.'

Ellen aimed the flashlight at four men's watches, a couple of women's rings, and a bracelet. 'Not a bad little take,' she said. 'Worth a couple grand, I'd guess.'

'No surprise. Staff's, probably. Kiefer's been running around in scrubs. Looking like a doctor, he had easy access to every washroom in the building. Let it be, prints and all. We'll get somebody back here after it later.'

He heard the commotion, the burst of static, before he heard his page.

'Sellers. What's up?'

'Slimy little bastard, he slipped by Cox on four, but now he's back in the stairwell. When he finds out there's no exit downstairs, he may be on his way back up.'

Paul nodded. 'Good,' he said. 'Get someone at the stairwell on every floor. Keep him running till he drops from exhaustion or decides to come out quietly.'

It was raining hard again, slick sheets of water cascading over the eaves. Margie stood at the top of the steps and looked out into the parking lot.

Paul would undoubtedly be upset that she'd needed to leave the building. For that matter, she was angry with herself for not parking closer to the entrance. But it wouldn't take long and she wouldn't melt, even if she did get wet. She'd be back in the hospital and get the report faxed out before it was time to meet Rob.

Opening the umbrella, she ran down the steps and turned toward the rear lot, but the canyon winds blew rain in her face and she found herself having to squint. She lowered the umbrella and bent into the wind, but then she couldn't see where she was going and icy water sprayed her ankles every time she passed through a puddle.

Trying to judge the distance to her car, she held the umbrella to one side. There was the Honda, a few more feet. She held the umbrella down. But when she looked up again, all she could see was a blinding flash of light.

They were playing with him, damn them all! Cops on every landing, leering at him through the glass, like he was some kind of rat in a trap.

Come and get me! Denny raged silently, running, pain searing his lungs. Up and down, up and down, panting, fighting for air.

Cops everywhere, damn them all! Where did they get my picture? He began to cry, scalding tears blending with the salt of his sweat. That's when he knew. It was over. He was finished. There was no place left to go.

He rested for a minute at the top of the stairs, his heart heaving in his chest. Then he pushed open the door to twelve and he saw them, a man and a woman.

He wanted to tell them they weren't so smart. Not any of them. Not so smart. He'd made a mistake. One mistake. He'd played this gig too long. He wanted to tell them they never would have caught him if he hadn't stuck around so long. He wanted to tell them...he wanted...he wanted...but he couldn't seem...to catch his breath...

'Sit down, Kiefer.' The big cop moved toward him. 'I've been wanting to talk to you.'

Margie blinked at the sudden glare. A flashlight, shining in her face!

She moved aside, but the light moved with her, blinding her, making her angry.

'What—?' she began, aware of the rain dripping off the edge of her umbrella.

'Who are you, please? What do you want?' Her heart began to pound.

The voice was harsh. 'Don't matter who I am. I know who *you* are, Marjorie.'

Fear shot through her, like live wires, and slowly ebbed away. This was it, then. No more warnings. She squeezed her eyes shut against the light.

'Marjorie Reed,' the voice went on. 'Ain't even *Doctor* Reed, is it? But you play like you are one and the judge listens. The judge, he listens real good.'

She tried to place the disembodied voice, her mind beginning to race. Paul was on his way. He would look for her soon. She had to keep this maniac talking.

'Who are you?' she shouted into the rain. 'What do you want me to do?'

'You done enough, Marjorie Reed. You and your lawyer boyfriend. But there ain't a nuthouse big enough to hold me. I figured a way out.'

A way out. Out of the nuthouse. You and your lawyer boyfriend... The pieces began to fall into place and the name came to her lips.

He must have seen the look of horror on her face, because suddenly he began to laugh—a low, guttural, disembodied cackle, muffled by the wind and the rain.

'Mr Gates,' she managed. 'Roy Gates.'

'Bingo! You get the prize. But you didn't

get the lawyer. I got him first. Quick. Too quick. Almost wasn't any fun.'

My God, he killed Frank! Margie swayed, fighting the urge to run. She was sickened, and blinded by the beam of his flashlight, but one thing she knew for certain. What she did next—and what she said—would determine whether she lived or died.

Kiefer lay at his feet, whimpering. Paul looked down in disgust. Ellen had barely recited the Miranda warning when the man had started spilling his guts.

'Get up, Kiefer.' He reached for the cuffs. 'Let's take a ride to the sheriff's station. You can talk there. I know somebody else who'll be wanting to talk to you, too.'

Kiefer got to his feet slowly. Ellen turned to Paul. 'I'll call Ray Nance in Santa Barbara as soon as we get him in. I have a feeling he's going to want to come down, rainstorm notwithstanding.'

Paul nodded, looking at Kiefer. 'I should have figured you were in here. I should have known it the other night, when we found that message on Margie's car.'

Kiefer blinked.

'The painted *X*! The red paint on the trunk—' He looked at Kiefer, looked straight at him, and the colour drained from his face. Margie had been right.

306

This pitiful wretch didn't have that kind of cunning.

He snatched up the radio. 'Fernandez, get up here! Wallace! Are you there?'

'Yes, sir.'

'Go to the auditorium on the main floor. Look for a Marjorie Reed.'

Margie shivered in the damp air, but she knew it was only from the cold. 'You're very clever,' she shouted into the rain. 'Leaving me all those messages. The slashed tyre, that was nothing. Anyone could have done that. But the funeral wreath—that was clever. How did you think of that?'

A pause. 'I was there, at your place, that night. I heard that woman scream. When I saw some dude take off like a bat, I figured I'd best get outta there. Then I heard on the news that the woman was dead. That's when I thought of the flowers.'

Keep him talking, Margie thought, praying that Paul would come soon, that someone, anyone, would see them like this and know that something was wrong.

'And the doll,' she said, the rain beating down, her head throbbing from the glare. 'I was very frightened. But you knew I would be. You knew that would scare me to death.'

She wished she could see him, could

see Gates's face. She had to gamble that he would respond; that he, like Glenn Walters, wanted her respect—needed her open admiration. When he didn't answer, she started to speak again, but all at once, the glaring light shifted. She saw the glint of metal. A knife. No! A gun. It was a gun. She felt her heart begin to race.

'Margie!'

From a distance she heard her name, and she whirled, confused. 'Rob?' Panic gripped her. Where had he come from? 'Rob! Rob, go back!'

But her brother kept running, coming closer, and she heard the crack of gunfire.

She heard herself screaming into the wind and the rain. She was running, stumbling, falling. She felt the tattoo of the rain on her face. Then she felt nothing at all.

CHAPTER 31

Margie felt as though she were fighting her way up through layers of cotton batting, and the more she pushed, the higher she climbed, the denser the layers became.

Her arms felt heavy and her legs, especially her right leg, seemed to be encased in cement.

From time to time she heard muffled voices, voices she did not recognize. There were bits of phrases—tarsus, trauma, transient loss of consciousness—and it occurred to her that she might open her eyes and try to make some sense of them. But the effort seemed somehow Herculean, and so she lay there, drifting, floating.

Then she heard a voice she thought she knew. Paul. Yes, it was Paul. When she opened her eyes it was his face she saw, and it filled her with elation.

She tried to sit up, but she felt dizzy, and Paul pushed her gently back down.

'Easy, tiger.' His voice was soft. 'Everything's going to be fine.'

Confused, she looked around the room, and her mind seemed to flash backward—the confrontation, the relentless rain, the glare of the light, the gunshot.

'Rob!' Again she tried to raise herself up and her lips formed the single word.

Paul must have seen the anguish in her face. He brushed back her hair and shushed her. 'Rob is fine. He will be fine. He took a bullet in his left side. It was only a flesh wound, nothing serious. He's right down the hall from here.'

She lay back, afraid to ask more, and tried to shift her position. She could not seem to move her right leg. She looked at Paul with alarm.

'A broken ankle,' he told her softly. 'You slipped and fell in the rain. They've set it in a cast. And you hit your head. The doctors want to keep an eye on you.'

As if to give credence to what he was saying, a nurse entered the room—a frosted blonde with a wide smile and nearly perfect teeth. 'Well,' the nurse chirped. 'We're awake, are we? Good! Let's have a look.'

She asked Margie silly questions, like what was her middle name, what had she eaten for dinner last night, what month and year it was.

They were the kinds of questions you asked someone if you were checking for a concussion. Margie answered in a voice she hardly recognized—more a croak than a voice.

The nurse rewarded her with a big smile. 'You have a sore throat. Nothing to worry about. And your temperature's been a little elevated.' She whipped out an electronic thermometer. 'Here, let's try it again.'

While she waited for the temperature to register, she took Margie's pulse and nodded.

'Good girl,' she said, as though Margie had arranged it. 'Dr Soong will be happy to know you're doing fine.'

Flashing another generous smile, she

turned and left the room, leaving behind the scent of wildflowers and a deep, uneasy silence.

Paul looked at Margie. 'It's late,' he said. 'You need to get some rest.'

She shook her head. 'Gates. Where is Gates?'

'We've got him. We've got him in custody.' He looked at her, his eyes pleading. 'Margie, I'm the world's biggest jerk. My stubbornness could have...you were right. I was wrong. It was never Kiefer who was stalking you.'

She frowned. 'But Kiefer—it *was* Kiefer I saw at Santa Clarita?'

'Yes.' Paul took a deep breath and looked at her uncertainly. 'Margie, it's been a long night. Are you sure you're up to all this?'

She nodded as vigorously as she could manage, and he pulled his chair closer to the bed.

'Dennis Kiefer was holed up in the hospital, masquerading as a doctor. We found him, thanks to you, and we've got him in custody, too, charged, at the moment, with the murders of Jeanne Kerns and Emma Danziger. If I don't miss my guess, he'll also be charged with the murder of Ramon Garcia, a gardener from Santa Barbara, where Kiefer holed up before he came to Santa Clarita. He may end up being charged with a string of murders up and down the coast.'

Margie nodded. 'Gates was there, lurking around outside of my apartment the night that Kiefer murdered Jeanne. He told me that. That's when he decided to have some fun with me...'

'Margie—'

'There's more.' She blinked away tears. 'It was Gates who killed Frank. He told me that, too. It wasn't a thief. It was Gates in that country store.'

She did not know when Paul had taken her hand, but now she felt him squeeze it—slowly, tentatively, but with such tenderness that the tears sprang to her eyes, and he reached across her with his other hand and gently wiped them away.

A dozen questions whirled in her brain. Did Rob know Gates had killed Frank? How had Gates broken into her apartment—and how had he been taken into custody? But she was tired, suddenly so tired that she could not form the words, and she felt herself drifting back, back, into the layers of cotton...

Her ankle throbbed, and she seemed to drift somewhere between sleep and wakefulness. When she saw Rob's face staring down at her, she thought for a moment she was dreaming.

But it *was* Rob, pale, but standing,

supporting himself on crutches. 'They've got him, Marg,' he said evenly. 'Frank's killer. Paul has him in custody.'

Margie struggled to sit up. 'I know. Oh, Rob, you're all right. I remember—I remember you were running toward me, and then I heard the gunshot.'

Rob sank heavily into a chair, the crutches clattering to the floor. 'I knew who he was the minute I saw him. The minute I saw his face...'

'But how—?'

'I got finished with Chet earlier than I figured, and I went downstairs to find you. When I didn't see you in the auditorium, I decided to head for the car. I saw you standing there, and this guy with the flashlight, and I knew you were in trouble. Then I saw his face—I told you once, that face was burned into my brain—and I went berserk. I don't know what would have happened if Paul hadn't been right behind me.'

Margie stared. 'Do you know what you did? Rob, that bullet was meant for me.'

Rob shrugged, looking down at his lap. 'I know. But I had no choice.'

'What are you talking about?'

'Margie, please—I have to tell you something. Something that's been driving me nuts for months—ever since the night Frank died...'

Margie opened her mouth to speak, but Rob put a hand over her mouth.

'Please,' he said. 'I lied to you, Margie. I lied to the police the night Frank died. I knew that wasn't some gun-crazy thief who came into that store. He came in yelling Frank's name, and I never even tried to help—'

Margie winced. 'Did Frank know who it was?'

Rob shook his head. 'I don't know. He turned around when he heard his name. I did, too, of course.' He swallowed hard and looked away. 'But I ducked when I saw the gun.'

Margie waited, her eyes wide, her heart breaking for her brother. She had to let him say it, whatever it was—it had poisoned him long enough.

Rob looked up with tears in his eyes. 'I chickened out, Marg. I should've tried to help. Maybe I could have. Even the grocery clerk tried. But then he got shot—I heard him scream, and I just—I just hid there and prayed... I laid there, shaking, hiding behind a display case, and I prayed he wouldn't come after me.'

Now she tasted her own tears and she reached out for her brother, hugging him, feeling their tears mingle, feeling his racking sobs.

'Rob,' she murmured, 'there was nothing

you could have done. You had a wife—a pregnant wife! If you had died, too, you would have left her widowed, and it wouldn't have helped to save Frank.'

Rob shuddered. 'That's what I told myself. But I know I didn't believe it. That's why I couldn't ever face Trisha without feeling like a coward. And you, Marg—when you moved away, I was glad...and I hated myself even more...'

Margie held him, as she had when they were children, as if she could heal all his hurts. 'Frank would be the first one to tell you you did the only thing you could. You protected yourself—and your wife and your child. There was nothing you could have done for him...'

They huddled in silence for a long moment. Then Rob pulled away. 'I spilled it all out to Chet last night... I guess I'd just held it in too long... And then I told Trisha. I hope she understands—even if she married a coward.'

'You're not a coward, Rob. You never were. You proved that last night.'

Rob gave her a lopsided smile. 'Maybe. I don't know what I was thinking. If Paul hadn't appeared out of nowhere, we might have both been killed.'

Margie sighed, trying to make sense of it, knowing what he said was true. Gates would have killed her, as he'd killed

Frank, after his games had worn thin. She frowned. 'Rob. You were Frank's friend. Did it seem to you that he was worried?'

Rob looked puzzled.

'Toward the end,' she pressed. 'Did he ever think he was being threatened?'

Rob thought for a moment. 'I don't think so,' he said. 'It would have taken a lot to scare Frank. I remember when he got that stupid little trinket—the one you've got hanging from your key chain?'

The trinket on her key chain. Yes, of course. The one they'd found in Frank's pocket.

'Where did it come from?'

'Frank found it on his doorstep. He showed it to me and laughed. He said it was some kind of Indian token...some kind of Indian bogeyman.'

Margie sank back into her pillows. So Gates had left at least one warning. She closed her eyes. The pattern rarely changed. And it would have been like Frank to laugh it off.

She felt the last of her energy draining. 'I love you, Rob,' she managed.

'I love you, too.'

She heard him rooting around for his crutches as she drifted back into sleep.

She heard the voice, and it startled her

awake, a smooth, velvet baritone. Soon she recognized the song. McCartney. Lennon...yes. She lay there, listening, and after a moment the words played on her lips...

'I want her everywhere
and if she's beside me I know I need never care.
But to love her is to meet her everywhere knowing that love is to share;
each one believing that love never dies, watching her eyes and hoping I'm always there...'

Smiling, she let the voice caress her, and she waited till the song was through.

'You're a man of many talents,' she said.

Paul smiled. 'I thought you were sleeping.'

She felt his presence like the pull of gravity. 'I didn't know you could sing.'

He leaned toward her. 'No surprise. There are a lot of things about me you don't know.'

'Mmm,' she said, her face close to his. 'Lucky for you...I learn fast.'

The publishers hope that this book has given you enjoyable reading. Large Print Books are especially designed to be as easy to see and hold as possible. If you wish a complete list of our books, please ask at your local library or write directly to: Magna Large Print Books, Long Preston, North Yorkshire, BD23 4ND, England.

This Large Print Book for the Partially sighted, who cannot read normal print, is published under the auspices of

THE ULVERSCROFT FOUNDATION